Grace shifted uncomfortably. "I believe you've more than proven your point."

Cesar continued to look down at her for several long, tense seconds, as his usual reserve warred with the increasing need he felt to taste the fullness of Grace Blake's mouth.

She was his employee, damn it, and a young woman who had simply accompanied her employer to Buenos Aires for the sole purpose of cooking and serving dinner this evening. A beautiful and desirable young woman, but Cesar's employee, nonetheless.

"So I have," he rasped, his jaw tight as he pushed away from the wall to step back as the lift came to a halt and the doors opened to allow them to step out into the cool entrance hall of his apartment.

Grace followed him slowly on legs that felt decidedly shaky, sure that she must have been mistaken about that brief flare of hunger she thought she'd seen in Cesar Navarro's eyes a few seconds ago as he looked down at her mouth with those jet black eyes; it was more likely to have been displeasure rather than desire.

BUENOS AIRES
Nights

After dark with Argentina's most infamous billionaires!

Cesar Navarro and Raphael Cordoba—two Argentineans with the wealth, magnetism and ruthlessness to break many a woman's heart.

Grace and Beth—two ordinary British women about to make their first foray into the sultry heat of Buenos Aires nights.

Read all about Grace and her boss, Cesar, in

A TASTE OF THE FORBIDDEN

April 2013

Read Beth and bodyguard Raphael's story:

A TOUCH OF NOTORIETY

May 2013

Carole Mortimer

A TASTE OF THE FORBIDDEN

BUENOS AIRES
Nights

HARLEQUIN PRESENTS®

Recycling programs
for this product may
not exist in your area.

ISBN-13: 978-0-373-13136-5

A TASTE OF THE FORBIDDEN

Copyright © 2013 by Carole Mortimer

HARLEQUIN®
www.Harlequin.com

Printed in U.S.A.

All about the author…
Carole Mortimer

CAROLE MORTIMER is one of Harlequin's® most popular and prolific authors. Since her first novel, published in 1979, this British writer has shown no signs of slowing her pace. In fact, she has published more than 135 novels!

Her strong, traditional romances, with their distinct style, brilliantly developed characters and romantic plot twists, have earned her an enthusiastic audience worldwide.

Carole was born in a village in England that she claims was so small that "if you blinked as you drove through it you could miss seeing it completely!" She adds that her parents still live in the house where she first came into the world, and her two brothers live very close by.

Carole's early ambition to become a nurse came to an abrupt end after only one year of training due to a weakness in her back, suffered in the aftermath of a fall. Instead, she went on to work in the computer department of a well-known stationery company.

During her time there, Carole made her first attempt at writing a novel for Harlequin. "The manuscript was far too short and the plotline not up to standard, so I naturally received a rejection slip," she says. "Not taking rejection well, I went off in a sulk for two years before deciding to have another go." Her second manuscript was accepted, beginning a long and fruitful career. She says she has "enjoyed every moment of it!"

Carole lives "in a most beautiful part of Britain" with her husband and children.

Other titles by Carole Mortimer available in ebook:

Harlequin Presents®

For my beautiful and loving Mum—I admire you
so much—and for my wonderful Dad,
my own first and forever hero.
I love you both so very much.

CHAPTER ONE

'Now, YOU'RE SURE you're going to be okay here on your own?'

'Grace, will you stop worrying and just get in your car and drive!' Her sister, Beth, shot her an affectionate but impatient glance. 'I'm twenty-three years old, not three, and perfectly capable of living on my own. Besides, we need the money…'

Yes, they did, Grace acknowledged, only too well aware that the bills, which had accumulated during the last six months of their mother's illness—when Grace had had to give up her job as pastry chef in one of London's leading hotels so that she might stay with their mother constantly, and so allowing Beth to finish her Master's degree at Oxford University—were still waiting to be paid.

Admittedly Beth had now moved back to the family home, and had a job in London working at a reputable publishing company, but there was no way that her wage alone could support the two of them and pay those accumulated bills.

Which was why Grace was now on her way to the wilds of Hampshire for the trial period of one month, with a view to becoming the permanent cook/housekeeper at the English home of a mega-rich Argentinian businessman. Presumably, as Grace would be based in Hampshire, Cesar

Navarro employed other permanent cook/housekeepers in the properties he owned in so many other parts of the world…? Although goodness knew what they were supposed to do with themselves when he wasn't in residence!

'I wonder what Cesar Navarro is like in the flesh?' Beth added speculatively, echoing some of Grace's own thoughts.

Grace gave a snort as she looked up from checking the contents of her cavernous shoulder bag. 'I very much doubt I'm going to get the chance to meet the man himself any time soon!'

Her younger sister gave a frown. 'What do you mean?'

Anyone looking at the two of them, Beth, tall, blonde and dark-eyed, and Grace just a little over five feet tall with long dark hair and blue-green eyes, would probably have no problem realising that the two women weren't actually biological sisters.

Grace had been adopted when she was only six weeks old, and had remained an only child until she was eight years old, when her adoptive parents had brought five-year-old Beth home and introduced her as her new sister. It had been love at first sight for the two little girls, and thankfully it had been that love and affection that had supported the two of them after their adoptive father died in a car crash four years ago, which had left their mother paralysed and in a wheelchair for the rest of her life. It had been chest complications brought on by that immobility that had finally killed her two months ago.

Grace gave a rueful grimace. 'According to his London PA, who, as you know, interviewed and employed me—once I had passed the stringent security check, apparently!—I am to make sure breakfast is ready for his man, Raphael, to take up to the dining-room at seven o'clock each morning. Remain out of the main part of the house until after Mr Navarro has left for the day, after which time I'm allowed to clear away and tidy the house—though not his study, apparently, which is totally out of bounds—ready for his return that evening.

'Evenings will follow the same routine—unless Raphael informs me otherwise, dinner is to be ready for serving promptly at eight o'clock. And finally I have to be out of the house by nine o'clock each evening—after which time it's no doubt, party, party, party!'

'Do you really think so?'

'No.' Grace grimaced. 'What I think is that the arrogant Mr Navarro doesn't want to accidentally catch sight or sound of anyone as lowly as the domestic staff!'

Beth gave a chuckle. 'He does sound a little…over the top in regard to his privacy.'

'With his billions he's probably used to getting exactly what he wants when he wants it.' And beggars couldn't be choosers; despite having excellent references from her last employer, Grace had found it difficult to secure another job as a pastry chef in London this past six weeks of looking, most places put off by the fact that she hadn't worked for almost eight months. Out of desperation Grace had finally signed on with an agency, and been offered this month's trial employment—very well-paid trial employment!—at Cesar Navarro's estate in Hampshire.

'Mmm.' Her sister grinned. 'But you do get your own cottage in the grounds of the estate to live in.'

'Just another way of ensuring Mr Navarro's privacy, I expect,' Grace dismissed ruefully.

'Never mind, sis, I'll pop down one weekend and keep you company for a couple of days,' Beth consoled.

'I have a feeling I'm going to need company by that time!' She gave a husky laugh as she gave Beth a final hug before leaving. 'In the meantime, you'll call me on my mobile if you need me…?'

'By the sounds of it you might be the one who needs to call me—often!' Beth gave a rueful shake of her head.

Grace thought over those unusual demands of her future employer as she made the drive down to Hampshire. She had heard of Cesar Navarro, of course—who hadn't heard of the multibillionaire Argentinian businessman, aged in his early thirties, who not only had homes in most of the capitals of the world, but also seemed to own half the businesses in that world? Well…maybe half the world was a slight exaggeration—a quarter was probably more realistic!

His empire included high-tech businesses, extensive media, airlines, property, hotels, vineyards—the man seemed to have a finger in so many pies Grace wondered how he ever found the time to do anything but work.

Maybe he didn't?

Having had to wait a couple of days to hear whether or not she was being offered a second interview—while that security check was being carried out, no doubt!—Grace had gone online and looked up information on the elusive Mr Navarro.

Reclusive probably better described him, she had realised after reading the little information there was available on him; aged thirty-three, the eldest of the two children born to his wealthy and now separated American mother and Argentinian father, he had grown up in his father's country, then gone on to Harvard University before establishing his own business at the age of twenty-three.

A business empire that had now grown to such mega proportions it necessitated Navarro travelling extensively in his private jet or helicopter, and staying exclusively in those private homes he owned all over the world when he did so.

There had been several photographs on the website of when he was younger, revealing him as being a strikingly handsome youth. Even then his face had been all harsh aristocratic angles—piercing dark eyes, high cheek-bones, and sculpted lips, with a square jaw and deter-mined chin. But, without exception, every one of those photographs had shown his swarthy face as being grim and unsmiling.

There had been two photographs available of him as an adult, one obviously a posed photograph, and the other taken from a distance as he was stepping from his jet onto a helicopter at some private airfield—and in both he had looked just as strikingly handsome but even grimmer!

He had appeared an inch or two taller than the equally dark-haired man walking beside him across the tarmac, the darkness of his suit emphasising the width of muscled shoulders and a lean body, with overlong and slightly tou-sled very dark hair—from the wind of the rotor blades of the helicopter?—the harshness of his aristocratically hand-some features still dominated by those piercing dark eyes beneath equally dark brows.

Considering his incredible wealth, and those harshly hewn good looks, Grace couldn't understand why her fu-ture boss wasn't also the biggest playboy on the planet, photographed with a different beautiful woman on his arm every evening—a woman who would share the privacy of his bed later that night—rather than guarding his private life to the point of obsession in the way that he did.

Unless…

Maybe there was a reason Cesar Navarro had never been photographed with a beautiful woman on his arm? The same reason he kept his private life very private? And maybe that dark-haired man stepping onto the helicopter with him wasn't simply another one of his PAs, as Grace had assumed he must be?

Now wouldn't that be a crying shame: mega-rich, still single in his early thirties, with arrogant good looks enough to make any woman's heart flutter—and all for the private edification of another man!

Grace gave a chuckle at her wayward thoughts, only for that chuckle to slowly fade and be replaced by a frown as, having followed Kevin Maddox's instructions, she now found herself approaching the entrance to the estate where she was to live and work for at least the next month.

Huge wrought-iron gates were set in a surrounding wall that was at least twelve feet high, with two huge men dressed in matching black suits standing either side of them, their hair military-style short, their stances watchful, the expression in their eyes hidden by black reflective sunglasses—and the sun wasn't even shining on this overcast September day!

One of the men approached Grace's car as she braked in the driveway and wound down the window.

'Grace Blake?'

'Er—yes,' she answered uncertainly, relieved that she was expected, considering the level of security, but a little concerned as to the reason for that high security; she had been led to believe, in the telephone conversation she'd had with Kevin Maddox yesterday, that his Argentinian employer wasn't due to arrive in England until some time tomorrow…

The burly security guard gave a terse nod after checking out the back seat behind her. 'If I could just take a look in the boot of your car…?'

'The boot of my car…?'

'If you wouldn't mind.' He stood to one side as Grace

got out of the car and opened the boot for him. He insisted on checking the contents of her suitcase, too, before stepping aside to speak softly into the small radio attached to the lapel of his jacket, and seconds later the huge iron gates began to slowly open.

'The first turning to the right will take you to your cottage,' he instructed Grace abruptly before resuming his post beside the now open gates, his stance once again alert and watchful.

Grace edged the car forward until she was on a level with him. 'Er—I was told Mr Navarro wasn't arriving until some time tomorrow?' It would be just her luck to have arrived after her new employer!

His mouth tightened. 'No.'

'Oh.' She gave a puzzled frown. 'Is there usually this much security even when he isn't in residence?'

'Yes.'

'Oh,' Grace murmured again; she couldn't see it but she felt the coolness of the assessing gaze now levelled on her from behind those dark sunglasses. 'Okay. Thanks.'

'First turning on the right,' he repeated tersely, once again facing forward.

Grace's stomach gave a definite dip as she accelerated the car onto the driveway and saw the gates slowly closing behind her in the driving mirror. She felt, if she didn't see, the security cameras she was sure were now levelled on her as she drove slowly down the tree-lined driveway and turned to the right to approach the cottage Kevin had told her was to be her home for the next month, at least.

And Grace, totally used to doing what she wanted when she wanted, was already starting to have serious doubts that she would be able to live in this security prison for longer than that month's trial period...

* * *

'I will accept no excuses, Kevin,' Cesar rasped impatiently as he strode forcefully into the cavernous hallway of his English home the next day, a little tired after having worked for the whole of the flight over from Buenos Aires, and in no mood to deal with any setbacks in the deal he had flown to England especially to complete. 'If Dreyfuss does not— What are these?' He came to an abrupt halt beside the table standing in the middle of the hallway.

Kevin winced as he looked at the decorative vase of flowers. 'Er—lilies?'

Cesar's jaw tightened. 'The minute we finish our conversation I want them removed,' he snapped before continuing on down the hallway to his study.

'Of course.' Wisely, the other man didn't so much as question why as he trailed behind him.

Cesar waited until he was seated behind the huge mahogany desk in his study before pinning the younger man with the darkness of his gaze. 'I am sure I have made it more than clear that there are never to be flowers inside the house?'

Kevin grimaced. 'I apologise. I must have omitted to mention that to Miss Blake...'

Cesar arched a dark brow. 'The new housekeeper?'

'Mrs Davis retired—'

'I am well aware of that. I believe I gave her a cheque on her retirement.' The firmness of his mouth quirked derisively.

'Yes, you did,' Kevin confirmed, having been responsible for the delivery of that cheque. 'I obviously sent Miss Blake's file to Raphael for his approval.'

'Obviously.' Cesar nodded tersely. 'You have a copy of that file with you now?'

'Of course.' Kevin opened his briefcase and removed

the appropriate file before handing it to him. 'She's a little young but her references were excellent, and as I said, the security check on her panned out.'

Cesar opened the file, his brows rising as he immediately saw Grace Blake's date of birth placing her as being only twenty-six years old. 'A little young…?' He eyed Kevin speculatively.

Kevin looked uncomfortable. 'Her references were excellent.'

'So you said…' Cesar sat back in his chair and regarded the younger man with narrowed eyes. 'Is she also beautiful?'

Kevin flushed. 'If you think for one moment I would let the way she looks influence me—'

'So she is beautiful,' Cesar drawled mockingly. 'She also does not appear to have been employed for the past eight months…?' he added after another glance at the file.

'No. Well. Her mother was very ill, and so she gave up her job to nurse her—'

'I do not believe I asked for details of her private life, Kevin.' A nerve pulsed in the tightness of his jaw.

'I was merely trying to explain— No, of course you didn't.' The other man nodded as Cesar simply continued to look up at him. 'I'll talk to her about the flowers as soon as we've finished here.'

'See that you do.' Cesar's jaw was still tight as he closed the file on Miss Blake with a firm snap before putting it to one side to be read more thoroughly later.

Raphael was still outside bringing himself up to date in regards to the security here, but Cesar had no doubts that when the other man returned he would very quickly ensure that the young and beautiful Miss Blake knew exactly what Cesar would and would not accept from his employees.

* * *

Grace was putting the finishing touches to the dessert she was preparing for Cesar Navarro's dinner when Kevin Maddox strolled into the kitchen. 'How nice to see you again, Kevin,' she greeted him warmly.

She had heard the helicopter arrive about fifteen minutes ago, and had hoped that Kevin would have accompanied Mr Navarro. He was someone she considered as being relatively normal, after the past two days of feeling as if her every move were being watched, either from behind those reflective black sunglasses worn by the numerous security guards that constantly seemed to be on duty, or the cameras she had discovered both in the house and the grounds, and no doubt watched over intently by even more security guards in that room full of monitors she had discovered in the basement of the house when she went exploring earlier today!

The cottage she had been given to stay in was more than adequate, luxurious in fact, but the inside of the main house was breathtaking, with its elegant antique furniture and statuary, ornate ceilings and gleaming glass chandeliers, beautiful paintings—all originals, no doubt!—adorning the pale silk-covered walls.

As for the kitchen…!

If she ignored the two security cameras placed strategically in two corners of the room, and the fact that she had to key in a code to get in and out of the back door, then it was possible to appreciate that the mellow oak units gave the room an old-fashioned appeal, at the same time as it was a chef's delight, with every conceivable appliance necessary to produce the sumptuous cordon bleu meals she was expected to cook for its owner.

But getting in and out of the estate was every bit as much of a nightmare as Grace had thought it might be. As she had learnt when she went to shop for food in the nearest town this morning. Security out, security in, with all of the shopping bags being checked before the same guard from yesterday—Rodney, he had deigned to tell her was his name when she made a point of asking—would allow her and her car back inside the grounds.

Either Navarro was completely paranoid, or he had some really serious enemies. Neither of which possibility particularly appealed to Grace.

Kevin Maddox's homely good looks, short blond hair and deep blue eyes were like a breath of fresh air after only twenty-four hours of living in this goldfish bowl!

'Something smells good.' He nodded approvingly.

Grace nodded back, wearing her usual 'uniform' for working in: a crisp white blouse and pencil knee-length black skirt, with her long dark hair brushed back and secured in a ponytail so that it was out of the way as she prepared the food. 'Carrot soup, followed by grilled sea bass, minted new potatoes, with sautéed Mediterranean vegetables. And for dessert—'

'Ah.' Kevin gave a grimace as he looked down at the rich chocolate mousse Grace had been decorating with dark and white chocolate swirls when he entered the kitchen.

Her expression turned to dismay as she saw Kevin's expression. 'Mr Navarro doesn't like chocolate?'

'Mr Navarro doesn't eat dessert.'

Her eyes widened. 'What, none at all?'

'Nope.'

'But I specialised as a pastry chef!'

'I realise that.' Kevin shrugged. 'But you also did a cordon bleu cookery course in Paris before you specialised.'

'That isn't—' Grace broke off her impatient protest as she realised it was pointless; for the moment she needed this job, and if Cesar Navarro didn't eat dessert then he didn't eat dessert. 'Is there anything else Mr Navarro doesn't like to eat?' She picked up the glass dish of chocolate mousse and placed it in the refrigerator.

'I didn't say he doesn't like dessert, only that he doesn't eat it,' Kevin drawled ruefully.

'No doubt he's afraid of middle-aged spread— Sorry, I shouldn't have said that.' Grace sighed.

'No, you shouldn't,' Kevin agreed evenly. 'But while we're on the subject, he doesn't like the flowers in the entrance hall, either. Although, again, that's my mistake.' He grimaced. 'Mrs Davis was here long before I started working for Mr Navarro, and so knew of all his personal quir—preferences. I should have told you about them at our second interview,' he corrected his lapse briskly.

Grace frowned at Kevin Maddox. 'He doesn't like the lilies?'

'No.'

'Then what flowers does he like in the house?'

'He doesn't.'

She blinked. 'Does he have an allergy? Hay fever, something like that?' She knew how awful that could be—depending on the pollen count, her sister, Beth, could suffer dreadfully with hay fever during late spring and early summer, and then again in the autumn at harvest time.

'Not that I'm aware, no.'

Grace gave a frustrated shake of her head. 'Then what's not to like about having flowers in the house?' The long-stemmed pink lilies were absolutely beautiful, and they had smelt divine when she was arranging them in the vase earlier today.

Kevin shrugged broad shoulders. 'Experience has shown me that it's best never to question Mr Navarro's instructions.'

'When he says jump people just ask how high, hmm?' Grace guessed shrewdly.

Kevin gave a wry chuckle. 'That pretty much sums it up, yes.'

'And on this occasion he wants me to remove the flowers from the entrance hall?'

'Yes.'

'Okay.' She shrugged.

Kevin gave a sigh of relief. 'Apart from these few minor hiccups, how are you settling in?'

She wasn't. And now that Cesar Navarro had actually arrived, bringing yet more restrictions with him, she wasn't sure she wanted to, either...

The set of rules she had been given before she arrived, and the level of security once she had got here, were all alien enough, but Grace could actually feel Cesar Navarro's presence in the house now. A dark and arrogantly brooding presence that seemed to pervade the entire estate. Kevin Maddox certainly wasn't as relaxed and congenial as he had seemed at their two interviews, or during their telephone conversation yesterday, and no doubt Rodney, and his group of security cronies, were on even higher alert now that their boss was in residence.

How did people live in this way? How did Cesar Navarro live this way? Constantly shielded, in a protective bubble, set apart from the real world? Grace had no idea, but it certainly wasn't a lifestyle she would ever want for herself. Not that she would ever be rich enough, or important enough, to need to bother!

She gave Kevin a bright, noncommittal smile. 'The cottage is lovely, and this kitchen is amazing.' She looked about her appreciatively.

'That's good.' He nodded, obviously pleased with her answer. 'Raphael will be down shortly to check on Mr Navarro's dinner.' He gave a glance at his wristwatch as he straightened. 'Time I was leaving.'

'You don't stay here when Mr Navarro is in residence?' It was impossible for Grace to keep the disappointment from her tone.

Kevin shrugged. 'No one ever stays in the main house but Mr Navarro and Raphael.'

Mr Navarro and Raphael?

'Is Raphael just over six feet tall, with a masculine build, probably aged in his late twenties or early thirties, with dark hair and blue eyes?' she prompted, describing the man she had seen with Navarro in that photo.

'That pretty much describes him, yes,' Kevin confirmed cheerfully. 'How did you—? Ah, here he is now...' He turned as the other man entered the kitchen.

Yes, it was indeed that same dark-haired man.

Mr Navarro and Raphael.

Maybe Grace's previous thoughts on that subject weren't too far off the mark, after all?

Oh, well, live and let live had always been Grace's motto; two of her closest female friends in Paris had been a couple. In fact, they still were, the three of them having kept in regular contact since Grace had returned to England four years ago.

Not that Grace had chance to learn anything more about Raphael, or their employer, once Kevin had introduced the two of them and then taken his leave.

Raphael was kept busy going efficiently to and fro between the kitchen and the dining-room during the next hour as he served Cesar Navarro himself, the sternness of his expression not encouraging after the first couple of times Grace had tried to engage him in conversation and received only a grunt in reply.

Consequently, by the time Raphael gathered up the silver tray on which Grace had put the pot of strong black coffee—Navarro's personal brew, brought with him from Argentina, of course!—she was feeling more than a little exhausted, from all of her work today, as well as the strain of trying to engage the taciturn Raphael in conversation. So much so that she didn't even demur when Raphael curtly told her she was dismissed for the evening as he left the kitchen with the coffee tray.

Grace felt too weary to leave immediately, instead sinking down onto one of the four stools about the cream marble-topped breakfast bar. If this evening's tension, along with that restrictive security, was an example of how the next month was going to be, then she didn't think she was going to make it through the trial period. No matter how good—or welcome—the pay was!

CHAPTER TWO

'*Dios mio!*'

Grace shot to her feet at the first sound of that harshly surprised voice, feeling the colour draining from her cheeks as she looked across the shadowed darkness of the kitchen at the tall and imposing—and instantly recognisable!—figure of Cesar Navarro. He stood silhouetted in the kitchen doorway, those equally recognisable black eyes glittering across at her with piercing intensity.

Having finally recovered after Raphael had dismissed her, Grace had decided not to return to her lonely cottage just yet but to wash and clear away the last of the dinner things, rather than having to deal with them first thing in the morning.

Against her boss's instructions, she now realised.

Instructions that Kevin had informed her no one ever questioned—or disobeyed?

To make matters worse, she had once again been sitting at the breakfast bar, this time with only the light on over the cooker to break the stilled darkness, and enjoying the chocolate mousse Kevin had earlier told her Navarro didn't eat.

She swallowed hard. 'Mr Navarro...'

'Miss Blake, I presume?' His voice sounded dark and husky in the still of the night, his accent having a slightly

Transatlantic twang to it; no doubt courtesy of his American mother.

Grace ran the dampness of her palms down her black pencil skirt, wishing—oh, God, how she wished!—that she had gone back to her cottage as she was supposed to do. So much for her assertion to Beth of doubting she would set eyes on Cesar Navarro any time soon! As it was, Grace was probably not going to be given any choice about whether or not she wanted to complete the whole month's trial period.

'I—' She moistened the dryness of her lips. 'I have no excuse. I shouldn't be here. Kevin—Mr Maddox told me that I had to be out of the main house by nine o'clock, and Raphael dismissed me earlier. I just—it was still early, and I didn't want to go back to the cottage and be alone just yet, and I thought, or rather I decided to clear away so that I didn't have to do it in the morning,' she finished lamely.

Cesar had showered and gone to bed an hour ago, but having read through some business papers for that hour, he had then decided to come down to the kitchen for a glass of juice before going to sleep. He certainly hadn't expected to see the young woman Maddox had engaged as cook/housekeeper of his English home when he got there!

Grace Blake's file stated she was twenty-six years old, and yet she looked much younger than that as she stood in the beam of light given off by the single bulb over the cooker, standing only a little over five feet in height, her frame petite in a plain white blouse and black skirt. The sable darkness of her hair was pulled back and secured in a ponytail, leaving her ivory-skinned throat and make-up-less face fully exposed. And it was, as Cesar had guessed earlier this evening, a beautiful face: blue-green eyes surrounded by thick, dark lashes, with a sprinkling of freckles across the bridge of her short, straight nose and high cheekbones, her cheeks slightly hollow, as if she had recently lost weight, her lips a perfect bow above a stubbornly determined chin.

Cesar's mouth thinned as he stepped further into the dark shadows of the kitchen. 'Correct me if I am wrong, but you seem to be eating...chocolate mousse,' he drawled after glancing towards the glass bowl sitting on the breakfast bar, 'rather than clearing away?'

'Yes. Well.' Those ivory cheeks blushed prettily. 'I finished clearing away, and I—I had already made the mousse for your dinner before Kevin—Mr Maddox—told me that you don't eat dessert.'

He arched haughty brows. 'And so you decided to eat it yourself?'

'No! Well...yes.' She grimaced uncomfortably as the half full glass bowl on the breakfast bar mocked her denial. 'But only because I was feeling—' She broke off with a wince. 'Again, there's no excuse, and I apologise.'

'Because you were feeling...?'

'I'm used to living in London, you see, and the cottage is quite a distance from the main house, and on its own, and it's so quiet that I— Oh, to hell with this!' All the tension went out of the slenderness of her shoulders as she sighed heavily. 'Why doesn't someone just shoot me now and get it over with?'

Cesar's brows rose even higher. 'Shoot you?'

'Yes.' Grace Blake grimaced self-derisively. 'Just bring in Rodney, or one of his cohorts, and have them shoot me now.'

'You are referring to my chief security guard here?'

'If he's the same Rodney standing guard at the main gates, then, yes, that's him.' She nodded. 'I thought he was thawing towards me a little when I spoke to him earlier today, but I'm sure that if you were to tell him that I stole and ate your chocolate mousse, then he'll be only too glad to dispatch me—or whatever it is they call shooting some-one in security guard jargon.'

Cesar couldn't decide whether to laugh—something he did all too rarely—at this young woman's unusual and forthright manner, or do as she suggested, and call for Rodney—but only so that the other man might escort her back to her cottage in the grounds, rather than shoot her! 'You seriously think that Rodney would shoot you because you have eaten a chocolate mousse belonging to me?'

She grimaced. 'I seriously think he would do whatever you told him to do, no questions asked.'

Cesar hid his surprise at her statement behind hooded lids. 'I believe cold-blooded murder is illegal in this country.'

'Any sort of murder is illegal in this country,' she cor-rected pertly. 'But, with the level of security you have here, I doubt very much if you were to hide my body in the woods behind the house that anyone would ever find it.'

Cesar doubted very much that he had ever had a stranger conversation in his life. Strange, and yet somehow compel-ling at the same time. In as much as he had no idea what Miss Grace Blake was going to say next.

'You were about to tell me how you were feeling before you ate the chocolate mousse?' he prompted as he stepped fully into the beam of light.

Grace couldn't speak at all as she got her very first look at Cesar Navarro 'in the flesh', as Beth had put it. Good grief, the man was— Well, he was— The only word Grace could think of at that moment was *breathtaking*.

He was at least a foot taller than her own five feet three inches, the darkness of his overlong hair still in that rak-ishly tousled style—naturally so, judging from the slight wave in that midnight darkness—and those dark and glit-tering eyes were surrounded by the longest, thickest lashes

Grace had ever seen, on a man or a woman, his cheekbones high in that swarthy face, his nose thin and aristocratic, with sculpted lips—sexily sculpted lips!—above a square and determined jaw.

But it was probably what he was wearing—or, rather, what he wasn't wearing—that surprised Grace the most.

In the photograph she had seen of him he had been the height of understated—and, no doubt, expensive—elegance, in a perfectly tailored dark suit and white shirt, with a meticulously knotted silver tie at his throat. This evening he was dressed in a fitted black tee shirt that defined the muscled width of his shoulders and chest, leaving his equally muscled arms bare, and clinging to reveal the flat contours of his stomach—not an ounce of that middle-aged spread in sight!—with loose-fitting grey sweat-pants sitting low on the leanness of his hips, his long and elegant feet completely bare on the terracotta floor tiles.

Was he dressed for going to bed, or working out in the gym in the east wing of the house, which Grace had also discovered when she went exploring earlier today? He certainly didn't look all hot and sweaty, which he surely would have if it were the latter. Probably the former, too, if he hadn't gone to bed alone...

Whatever the reason for his casual clothing, his presence in the kitchen seemed to have sucked up all the air in the room, making it difficult for Grace to breathe, and his lean and muscled frame looked immense in the confines of the darkened kitchen, so much so that she felt sure he must rival in muscle any and all of the security guards he surrounded himself with.

'What a waste...' Grace heard herself murmur—and then winced as she realised she had spoken completely without thinking; just because she suspected that this man and Raphael were involved, there was no reason for her to say it out loud. In the circumstances, it was the last thing she should have said!

'Miss Blake?' Cesar prompted tersely.

'Nothing. Absolutely nothing.' She gave a firm shake of her head. 'What was I feeling before I ate the chocolate mousse?' she repeated desperately as she saw the way those dark eyes had narrowed speculatively. 'Homesick, if you really want to know, and a little lonely. And chocolate always has a way of making things seem a little less bleak, don't you think? No, of course you don't, because you don't eat sweet things. Why is that, by the way?' She looked up at him questioningly, and then wished she hadn't as she felt a decided click in her already tense neck.

Something that would become an occupational hazard if she had to stand and have too many conversations with this man. Which clearly wasn't going to happen, because he was going to have Rodney shoot her and hide her body in the woods—

And you're becoming hysterical, Grace, she admonished self-disgustedly. Unfortunately that realisation in no way helped to dispel those feelings, if her next comment was any indication, or the way in which she appreciatively eyed the muscled expanse of Cesar Navarro's chest when she made it. 'It certainly can't be because you're afraid of putting on unnecessary pounds.'

No, Cesar acknowledged ruefully, he really didn't have any idea what Grace Blake was going to say—or do!—next. Nor was he about to explain to this strange young lady that he had given up eating desserts because he considered them unnecessary frivolities. 'Did you perhaps drink some of my wine, too, this evening, in an effort to dispel those feelings of loneliness?'

'Certainly not.' She looked indignant at the suggestion. 'I rarely drink, and never when I'm at work.'

'I am glad to hear it,' he drawled dryly.

She blinked, obviously unsure as to whether or not he was being sarcastic. 'I'm just a little tired, that's all.'

And a lot emotional, was Cesar's guess.

He straightened. 'In that case, perhaps it would be better if we were to continue this conversation in the morning.'

Those blue-green eyes widened. 'Am I still going to be here in the morning?'

'As opposed to being "dispatched" and buried in the woods behind the house?' Cesar murmured softly.

Colour once again warmed her ivory cheeks. 'Maybe that was a little hysterical of me.'

He arched mocking brows. 'A little?'

Her eyes snapped with temper. 'Well, you would hardly have security guards here in the first place if you didn't intend for them to protect you, should the need arise!'

His mouth thinned impatiently. 'I do, however, draw the line at asking them to shoot outspoken cook/housekeepers. Even temporary ones,' he added abruptly.

'Oh.' Her guilty gaze dropped from meeting his as she obviously accepted that summary of her conduct so far this evening.

'Unless you are suggesting I might be in need of protection from you?'

Grace's breath had lodged somewhere in her throat as the sultry huskiness of his tone brought to mind—totally inappropriately!—thoughts of running her fingers up that broad and muscled chest to his tousled, just-had-sex hair, as she brought his mouth down to hers and—

Oh, good grief!

She must be feeling lonlier than she had realised if she was having thoughts of kissing Cesar Navarro, of all men. If she was having thoughts of kissing any man she had just met!

Oh, she'd had her share of boyfriends over the years, but none of those relationships had been in the least serious. She certainly hadn't been so bowled over by the sheer sensuality of any of those men that she had fantasised about kissing him within minutes of meeting him!

She wasn't fantasising about kissing her new boss, either! What would be the point, when his sexual inclinations obviously lay in a different direction?

'No, of course not,' Grace assured him briskly. 'As you say, perhaps it would be better if we finished this conversation in the clear light of day.'

He continued to look down at her with those brooding dark eyes for several long seconds, before slowly nodding his head. 'I will call for Rodney—so that he may escort you to your cottage, not "dispatch" you,' he snapped his impatience as Grace's eyes widened in alarm.

She breathed a sigh of relief. 'I'm quite capable of walking back to the cottage unescorted.'

His mouth tightened. 'It is late, and very dark outside.'

Grace grimaced. 'And there are so many security guards out there that there's no way anyone from outside could possibly get in and attack me!'

Cesar's eyes narrowed. 'You seem overly concerned by the presence of my security guards?'

'Perhaps just curious as to the need for so many of them?'

His mouth tightened. 'I am not in the habit of explaining myself. To anyone.'

'Least of all temporary employees.' Grace nodded. 'It's the cameras everywhere that give me the creeps.' She glanced up at one of those cameras in the corner of the kitchen, the pulsing red light showing that it was a live feed. 'You do realise that someone in the basement is watching the two of us right now?'

'But they cannot hear our conversation,' he assured her impatiently.

'Which is probably as well!' Grace grimaced. 'My remarks haven't exactly been polite,' she admitted ruefully as Cesar raised questioning brows.

No, this young woman's conversation had been far from the politeness he was used to, Cesar acknowledged derisively. So much so that he found Miss Blake's conversation strangely…refreshing, after years of stating his wants and needs and knowing they would be immediately satisfied; Grace Blake gave the impression she didn't do anyone's bidding unquestioningly.

As evidenced by the vase of pink lilies, which had adorned the table in the entrance hall earlier today, but which now stood in the middle of the kitchen table.

'It seemed a pity to waste them,' Grace defended quickly as she saw where the darkness of Cesar Navarro's compelling gaze now rested.

His jaw tightened. 'My instructions were for them to be—'

'Removed from the hallway,' Grace put in quickly. 'And, as you can see, I have removed them.'

'And instead placed them in the kitchen.'

'Well…yes.' Her cheeks burnt with colour. 'I only bought them this morning, and I couldn't bear to just throw them out when they're so beautiful. The perfume is absolutely divi—' She broke off as he continued to look steadily down the long length of his aristocratic nose at her. 'Maybe I could take them back to my cottage with me? Or would you consider that as stealing from you, too?'

'And, again, punishable by death?' he drawled dryly.

'I've already admitted I may have let my imagination wander a little on that one.' Grace winced at his obvious derision.

Cesar Navarro's expression was completely inscrutable as he turned to take the kitchen phone from its charger before pressing several buttons. 'I am merely calling Rodney so that he can escort— Rodney? Yes,' he bit out tersely into the receiver while the darkness of his gaze remained firmly fixed on Grace. 'No, there is no problem, but I would like you to escort Miss Blake back to her cottage. Yes, I am aware that should have been the case. Unfortunately Miss Blake seems incapable of following even the simplest of instructions.'

She gasped. 'That's hardly fair—'

'The kitchen.' Cesar completely ignored Grace's protest as he continued to talk to his English Head of Security. 'One minute? I am sure that Miss Blake and I will be able to amuse ourselves for that length of time,' he drawled before abruptly ending the call and putting the phone back on its stand before folding his arms over his muscled chest to once again look down the length of his nose at her.

Grace eyed him in frustration. 'How nice to know that Rodney now thinks I'm some sort of a security risk!'

Cesar raised one dark brow. 'And is Rodney's opinion of such importance to you?'

'It is when he's licensed to carry a gun!'

His mouth thinned. 'You are uncomfortable with that knowledge?'

She grimaced. 'I think intimidated might be a better way of describing it.'

Cesar had lived with this high level of security for more than half his lifetime, and rarely noticed it any more; he had certainly never considered how other people might react to being constantly under surveillance. Not that it mattered to him how Grace Blake felt about it; the security that surrounded him and his family was for a specific reason, and he had no intention of changing it to suit his English cook/housekeeper. His on-a-one-month's-trial English cook/housekeeper…

'Ah, Rodney.' He turned to look at the other man as he let himself quietly in by the back door. 'Miss Blake is ready to leave.'

'This really isn't necessary,' Grace Blake protested with obvious discomfort.

'I have already explained the reasons I consider it important—'

'Oh, well, that makes it all right, then!'

Cesar's eyes narrowed at her obvious sarcasm. 'Do not forget to take the lilies with you,' he reminded as she turned to follow the silent Rodney. 'Take the vase, too,' he added wearily as she attempted to remove the flowers and immediately dripped water all over the table top.

'I—thank you.' She quickly wiped the table before gathering the cut-glass vase up in her arms, and was instantly dwarfed by both its weight and the height of the flowers.

'Rodney?' Cesar gave the other man an exasperated glance.

'Yes, sir.' His English Head of Security was obviously having the same problem as Cesar had earlier as he took the vase of flowers out of Grace Blake's arms, in as much as it took great effort on his part not to laugh at her disgruntled expression. Evidence, perhaps, that Rodney was, as Grace Blake had thought earlier, thawing towards her?

Understandably so, perhaps, when not only was Miss Blake naturally beautiful, but her forthright way of talking was entertaining, to say the least.

'Goodnight, Miss Blake,' Cesar bit out dismissively as Rodney stood back politely in order to allow her to precede him out of the kitchen.

She turned slightly, her gaze not quite meeting his as she nodded. 'Mr Navarro.'

Cesar waited until she and Rodney had both departed the kitchen, the door locked securely behind them, before his mouth curved into a rueful smile at the strangeness of their encounter.

Grace Blake was not at all what he had been expecting of his newest employee. She was too young. Too beautiful. And far too outspoken!

There was no denying that she was an excellent cook, however; the meal she had prepared for him earlier this evening was as good as anything Cesar had ever eaten in any of the exclusive restaurants he frequented all over the world.

Speaking of which…

Cesar bent slightly to pick up the bowl of half-eaten chocolate mousse from the marble-topped breakfast bar, ignoring the teaspoon sticking out of it in favour of dipping the tip of one of his fingers into the thick concoction before bringing it up to his lips.

Only to give an involuntary groan as the richness of the deliciously creamy chocolate hit his taste buds, almost—but not quite!—with the same force of the physical pleasure experienced during sex.

Not that Cesar allowed himself to indulge in that luxury too often, either; he preferred to maintain tight control over all areas of his life, no matter what the cost to his personal comfort.

Nevertheless…

Another dip of the fingertip, a taste, another groan of ecstasy, and Cesar gave up all idea of leaving the kitchen before he had eaten every last temptingly decadent scoop of it.

'Come in, Miss Blake.'

Grace felt her tension rising as Cesar Navarro responded

dryly to her knock on the door to his study at eight-thirty the following morning. The do-not-ever-enter study that she had been summoned to just a few short minutes ago, when Kevin had sought her out in the kitchen for the sole purpose of telling her that Mr Navarro wanted to see her immediately.

Kevin had looked at her questioningly once he had passed on his employer's request, but if his boss hadn't confided in the other man regarding the details of their conversation in the kitchen the night before, then Grace wasn't about to do so, either.

Besides which, Kevin would find out soon enough what the meeting was about—when Cesar Navarro later informed him of her dismissal!

Grace had telephoned Beth last night as soon Rodney had left her alone in the privacy of her cottage, her sister unable to stop herself from chuckling as Grace related every embarrassing detail of that late-night meeting in the kitchen with Cesar Navarro.

Grace had chuckled wryly, too, once she got over feeling so embarrassed about the whole thing, only to wake up at six o'clock this morning in the full certainty that she was going to be dismissed at the first opportunity.

Obviously he had waited until after she had prepared his breakfast before finding that opportunity...

Grace checked that her hair was secured in its usual tidy ponytail, and smoothed down her black skirt, before quietly opening the door to the study and stepping gingerly inside. Only to come to an abrupt halt just inside the door of the wood-panelled study as she found herself looking across a huge mahogany desk at the same formal Cesar from that photograph she had seen of him online; he was wearing another impeccably tailored suit, in charcoal grey this time, with a snowy white shirt, and a meticulously knotted pale blue silk tie. Only that sexily tousled dark hair was reminiscent of the man she had met in the kitchen the previous night.

Probably not the best of things for her to have thought of when she had obviously been brought here so that he could tell her personally all the reasons why he had decided she was totally unsuitable to work for him!

'Did you personally make the croissants I had with my breakfast this morning?'

Grace blinked at the unexpected question. 'I—Sorry...?'

Cesar eyed her impatiently. 'I asked if you had made the croissants I ate for my breakfast earlier.'

'Er—yes.' Was this some sort of game? Grace wondered, feeling dazed. The one where you lulled your opponent into a false sense of security, and just when they were starting to relax you kicked them in the teeth? Because if so—

'They were delicious.' He nodded briskly. 'As good as anything I have tasted in some of the best hotels in Paris.'

So they should be, when Grace had worked in one of those hotels for over a year, under one of the best chefs in France, once she had completed her cordon bleu course.

'I'm pleased you enjoyed them.' She gave a shrug. 'Consider them a parting gift from me to you.'

Those piercing black eyes narrowed. 'You are leaving?'

'Of course I—' Grace eyed him warily. 'Isn't that why you had me brought here, so that you could have the pleasure of dismissing me personally?'

Cesar had wondered, after returning to his bedroom the previous night, if perhaps he had just met Grace Blake at a time when she was obviously feeling vulnerable and homesick, and resulting in that vulnerability making her more verbose than she might otherwise have been. Two minutes in her company this morning and he knew that was not the case; she really was this outspoken all of the time!

He arched dark brows. 'And why do you believe it would give me personal pleasure to dismiss you?' He arched dark brows as he studied her beneath hooded lids.

Those freckles across her nose and cheeks were more visible in the clear light of day, her eyes the beautiful clear colour of the Mediterranean Sea, neither blue nor green, but somewhere in between. Her hair was a rich shiny sable, but was unfortunately once again confined in a ponytail at her nape. Even so it was possible for Cesar to tell that it would probably reach almost to her waist once released.

She shifted uncomfortably beneath the steady implacability of his gaze. 'I was very outspoken last night. And rude. And maybe a tad sarcastic. And—' She broke off as Cesar slowly stood up before moving around his desk, deftly avoiding knocking the single framed photograph; sitting to one side of it, he leant against the front of the desk.

A photograph of Raphael, perhaps?

'And?' he prompted softly.

Her eyes were very wide and she swallowed before answering. 'And I expressed a dislike of the excessive security you have in place here.'

'Yes,' he drawled dryly.

She blinked. 'Yes, I was outspoken? Yes, I was rude? Yes, I was a tad sarcastic? Or yes, I expressed being uncomfortable with the excessive security you surround yourself with?'

'Yes, you did all four of those things,' Cesar confirmed tersely.

'There you go, then.' She smiled ruefully.

'There I go what?' he prompted irritably. Outspokenness was one thing, incomprehension was something else entirely.

Grace eyed him impatiently, more than a little overwhelmed by this man's close proximity. As she was also aware of how his sheer presence seemed to have once again sucked all the air out of the room. 'There are all the reasons you're going to dismiss me!'

'The reasons I am going to enjoy *personally* dismissing you was, I believe, the phrase you used?'

'Does it matter?' Grace gave a heavy sigh at his tenacity. 'The bottom line is that you're sacking me. The level of enjoyment you're going to feel from doing so irrelevant—'

'To you, perhaps,' he bit out coldly. 'I happen to take exception to being accused of enjoying depriving anyone of their employment.'

And that exception was clearly visible in the dark glitter of his eyes, thinned and disapproving mouth, and the nerve pulsing in his tightly clenched jaw!

'Okay, I'm sorry if— I was obviously mistaken. I spoke hastily. You may not enjoy doing it, but you're going to do it, anyway,' she substituted lightly.

If that was Grace Blake's idea of an apology then Cesar believed she needed to work on her people skills—because she had just succeeded in insulting him for a second time in as many minutes!

'Better yet,' she brightened. 'Why don't we just take it as said, I'll go back to the cottage and pack my things, and then be on my way? You and Raphael would probably appreciate not having a third party under your feet all the time, anyway.'

Cesar had the feeling that he had somehow lost control of this conversation some minutes ago. Not a normal occurrence for him: usually when he spoke people listened; they certainly did not attempt to speak for him!

He raised a frustrated hand to his chin as he eyed Grace Blake impatiently. 'Myself and Raphael…?'

'Don't worry, your secret is safe with me.' She reached out to place a reassuring hand on his sleeve-covered arm before quickly withdrawing it, a blush once again darkening her cheeks. 'Kevin had me sign some sort of privacy contract at the end of our second interview, anyway, no doubt so that you could sue me if I breathe a word to anyone about your private life.' She gave him another one of those bright smiles.

'Myself and Raphael,' Cesar repeated softly. Very softly. The sort of lethally laced softness that family and foes alike knew to beware of.

And which Grace Blake should be very wary of if her comments just now meant what Cesar thought they did!

CHAPTER THREE

ONE GLANCE AT THE COLDNESS in Cesar Navarro's glittering black eyes, and the harshness to his swarthy and chiselled features, and Grace knew that she had said something to annoy him.

Again.

He had that same stillness and coldness of expression that her father had always had when she or Beth had done something wrong; Clive Blake had been a wonderful and loving father to them both, one that never, ever raised his voice to his two daughters—because he hadn't needed to, just that cold stillness enough to tell them he was displeased or disappointed.

As Cesar Navarro's cold stillness now told her he was the former, at the very least!

Grace's feet seemed to be weighted down on the carpeted floor, and her mind had gone blank, making it impossible for her to either flee or remember what they had been talking about immediately before he became the iceman.

Ah, yes, she remembered now; she had been reassuring him as to her complete discretion in regard to his relationship with Raphael—

Oh.

Grace looked up at Cesar searchingly before slowly giving a pained wince. 'You and Raphael aren't a couple?'

One dark brow arched over those glittering black eyes. 'Perhaps you would care to explain to me why it is you ever thought that we were?'

Even his tone of voice was the same as their dad's, Grace acknowledged with another inward wince: soft and reasoning, pleasantly so—before he verbally remonstrated with them for whatever misdemeanour they were guilty of. Except, if her assumption concerning a relationship between Cesar and Raphael had been an incorrect one— and the chilling expression on his face clearly said that it was!—then this was so much worse than a misdemeanour.

If he hadn't been going to fire her before, then he certainly wasn't going to hesitate about doing so now.

Quite irrationally Grace found herself wondering who exactly was in that single framed photograph facing away from her on Cesar's desk. Obviously someone who mattered in his life; he wasn't the sort of man, was far too unemotional, too self-contained, to display a photograph on a whim.

None of which was helping her to find a suitable answer to his question. 'It seemed the likeliest explanation for why a young, mega-wealthy and gorgeously handsome man in his prime hasn't been photographed in the newspapers with the hordes of beautiful women he takes to his silk-sheeted bed every night—' Grace broke off with a gasp as she realised she had just made the situation worse, not better. 'I can't believe I said any of that out loud!'

'I assure you that you did.' Again, Cesar was unsure of how he felt about the directness of this woman's remarks, had no idea whether he should put an end to this now and simply ask her to leave—that decadent chocolate mousse aside!—laugh, or simply put her over his knee and give her curvaceous little bottom the smacking it deserved! 'And did it not occur to you that no such photographs exist because I happen to own, or have influence over, much of the media?'

'Ah.' She gave a grimace. 'Never thought of that. Does that mean that there are hordes of—'?

'Might I suggest that now might be a good time for you to exercise some caution over the things you say out loud?' Cesar eyed her warningly.

The directness of her gaze shifted away from his. 'Sorry.'

He nodded at her grudging apology. 'So, you consider me to be a "gorgeously handsome man in my prime", do you, Miss Blake?'

Her cheeks flushed so red now that Cesar thought she might internally combust. 'Well, reasonably so,' she finally conceded awkwardly.

Cesar settled himself more comfortably against the front of the desk, arms crossed over his chest as he realised he was enjoying her obvious discomfort. 'I had not realised there were degrees to being "gorgeously handsome" or "in your prime"?'

'Will you stop repeating that as if—as if—?' She gave an impatient shake of her head. 'Is Rodney anywhere about?'

'So that he might take you out into the woods and "dispatch" you?'

'Exactly!'

There was no longer any choice about it; Cesar couldn't hold back the impulse he had to laugh at this outrageously outspoken young woman.

Grace's eyes widened as she heard the husky softness of his laugh, a rich and throaty sound that stirred something to life deep inside her, not a slow or tentative stirring but a roaring, ripping, breaking free of an emotion she had never experienced in her life before.

Desire.

Grace gave a soft gasp as wave after wave of heat swept over her from her head to her toes, lingering and remaining in the swelling of her breasts, the tips becoming aching and engorged with that searing heat, a fiery liquid gushing between the apex of her thighs, dampening her swollen folds.

It was at one and the same time the most pleasurable and yet the most uncomfortable feeling Grace had ever known in her life!

Pleasurable because of that aching and swelling in the most intimate parts of her body, but uncomfortable because it was the enigmatic and reclusive Cesar Navarro, of all men, a man so totally beyond her reach or understanding, who had incited that desire.

Achingly.

Heatedly.

Unbelievably!

Even worse than the utter futility of that desire was the fact that Grace knew, by the way his laughter slowly began to fade, and those glittering and coal black eyes now narrowed on her in speculation, that he was as aware of her unbidden feelings of desire as she was!

She drew herself up tautly. 'Look, for everyone's sake, can we just take it that you've dismissed me and let Rodney escort me off the premises—before I have chance to say anything else to embarrass myself?'

Cesar felt somewhat bemused. Not only was his employee forthright to the point of embarrassing herself, but all of that honesty came from between perfectly bowed and moistly parted lips. Extremely kissable lips, which, the longer he looked them, caused his shaft to harden and swell in burgeoning desire. Lips Cesar now found himself looking at intently as he became curious to know whether or not they tasted as delicious as the chocolate mousse he had unexpectedly devoured the night before—

Ni en pedo!

No way!

Grace Blake worked for him, and Cesar did not have personal relationships with the women he employed. Even ones he found as interesting and unpredictable—and, apparently, arousing—as he did Miss Blake!

Even if the flush to her cheeks, and the arousal of her nipples beneath her fitted white blouse, now seemed to imply she found him equally physically intriguing.

Which placed Cesar in the dilemma that he was also no longer certain it would be wise for him to put forward the suggestion that had occurred to him the night before.

'Mr Navarro?' She looked at him warily now.

Cesar straightened abruptly before moving to resume his seat behind the desk, effectively putting the width of that desk between them, at the same time as it hid the swell of his arousal. 'You appear to have made a somewhat…rocky beginning to your employment with me, Miss Blake—' He broke off as she gave a self-derisive snort. 'Exactly.' He nodded tersely. 'Perhaps, if you are agreeable, we should attempt to start again?'

What exactly did he mean by that? Grace mused ruefully. Rather than asking her to leave, was he willing to overlook all those embarrassing foot-in-the-mouth things she had said to him, both last night and again this morning, and allow her to continue working for him, after all? If that was the case, then perhaps she had misjudged him and he wasn't the ruthlessly single-minded—even cold-blooded?—businessman she had believed him to be before the two of them had met?

And even if he was willing to overlook her outspoken familiarity to date, that didn't mean he was really going to forget those embarrassing things she had said to him—especially that 'gorgeously handsome' remark!

Or that Grace was going to be able to forget her completely physical reaction to the unexpected sound of his laughter, either.

She gave a rueful shake of her head. 'I'm really not sure that I'm suited to living out in the wilds of Hampshire for any length of time.'

'This estate is hardly in "the wilds" of anywhere, Miss Blake,' he drawled. 'The nearest town is only ten point two kilometres away, and there are twenty other people living within the walls of the estate. Yes, I am aware that the majority of them are my security,' he added impatiently as Grace would have interrupted. 'But that does not make them any less other human beings to talk and relate to.'

Why was she not surprised that Cesar Navarro knew exactly how many kilometres it was to town, or the exact number of people there were working on his estate?

Grace gave a grimace. 'They, and the cameras everywhere, make me feel like a goldfish in a bowl.'

'The cameras are not everywhere, Miss Blake.' He frowned his irritation. 'There are none in the bathrooms, for example—'

'That would be totally paranoid!' she came back tartly. 'Besides being a total invasion of privacy,' she added.

'You believe me to be paranoid, Miss Blake?'

There was no missing the steely edge to his tone. 'I'm not used to having my every move watched—'

'There are no security cameras in here.'

'This is also the one room I'm barred from entering!'

'When I am not in it, yes,' Cesar conceded, still annoyed

at the 'paranoid' comment. 'When the study is empty the motion sensor alarm would go off if you were to enter.'

'Oh, great!' She eyed him derisively. 'What exactly do you have in here that's so valuable I'm not even allowed to come in and dust?'

Cesar breathed deeply through his nose. 'This is my sanctuary. Somewhere that I come for complete privacy.'

'To do what, exactly? Do you dance around the room naked on a full moon or something?'

Cesar's breath caught in his throat, not even the gleam of laughter he could see in those wide blue-green eyes enough to temper his rising incredulity with this woman. 'Do you ever stop to think before you speak?' he prompted softly.

'Usually.' She grimaced. 'For some reason, my filter button seems to be on "off" whenever I talk to you.'

He arched a brow. 'I make you nervous, perhaps?'

'That's an understatement!'

'Would you care to explain what it is about me that makes you nervous?'

Everything would be the answer to that question, Grace realised with dismay. Cesar Navarro was too big, too immediate, too arrogantly sure of himself, too self-contained, the latter to such a degree she was constantly filled with this overwhelming—and uncharacteristic—impulse to try to shock him out of that self-containment. And lastly, he really was too 'gorgeously handsome' for his own good.

She drew in a deep breath. 'I don't think so, no.'

Cesar's mouth quirked at the firm finality of her tone. 'Can it be that you are learning some discretion at last?'

She raised her eyes heavenwards. 'We can always hope so.'

He nodded. 'And to answer your previous question—

perhaps I just like the feeling of knowing that I could dance around the room naked if I wished to do so?'

'Really?' Grace looked taken aback.

Cesar gave a disgusted snort. 'This conversation really has become too ridiculous!' He gave an impatient shake of his head as he realised he was now trying to shock her, a dangerous game that could only become even more so.

'I asked to see you this morning because your comments last night, in regard to the isolation of the cottage where you are currently staying, led me to believe, if you are to remain in my employment, that perhaps you might feel more comfortable occupying one of the bedrooms in the east wing of the house rather than remaining in the cottage?'

Her eyes widened. 'You're asking me to move into the main house with you and Raphael?'

Cesar's mouth tightened at the memory of the relationship Grace Blake had believed he had with the other man. 'I am suggesting that you might feel less isolated if you were to occupy one of the bedrooms in the east wing of the main house,' he repeated firmly.

She frowned. 'That's a bit of a turnaround from Kevin's initial comment to me that "no one ever stays in the main house but Mr Navarro and Raphael", isn't it?'

'And was it this remark which helped to convince you that Raphael and I must be…a couple?'

'That, along with Raphael's less than friendly attitude towards me yesterday evening,' she recalled with a frown.

Cesar's mouth twisted into a humourless smile. 'It did not occur to you that perhaps Raphael's presence here in the main house, and his "less than friendly attitude", might be for another reason other than the one you have so obviously jumped to?'

'What other reason?'

'Think, Miss Blake,' he drawled.

She shrugged. 'Well…he's with you constantly. Deals with your personal things. Serves your food. Obviously views strangers with suspicion until proven otherwise.'

'And what does all of that suggest to you, Miss Blake?'

'That he's as paranoid as you are?'

Cesar's mouth tightened. 'I may have found some of your outspokenness amusing to date, Miss Blake, but I nevertheless suggest you have a care.'

What did it suggest to her? Grace puzzled ruefully. There was the obvious conclusion she had come to, of course—and which Cesar Navarro had very firmly squashed! So what other—? 'He's your personal body-guard!' she realised slowly.

'Well done, Miss Blake.' He gave a terse inclination of his head. 'Not only is Raphael my personal bodyguard, but he is head of all my security. Rodney, and others like him at my other properties around the world, report directly to Raphael.'

'Oh.'

'Indeed,' Cesar said. 'He is a black belt in several of the martial arts, and is also an expert marksman from the years he spent in the army.'

Grace Blake nodded slowly. 'That makes sense. Did he actually taste your food last night and this morning before serving it?' she prompted sharply.

'Now that would be paranoid, Miss Blake.' Cesar eyed her impatiently. 'Unless you are suggesting that perhaps there might be some necessity for him to do so in future?'

Her cheeks warmed. 'Er—no.'

'Good.' He nodded briskly. 'Now, I have some work to do this morning before I leave to spend the day in London. If you would care to give my suggestion regarding staying in the main house some thought, and let me know your decision later today?' he bit out with abrupt and cold dismissal.

Grace, having come to Cesar Navarro's study under the clear impression—conviction—she was about to receive her marching orders for her outspoken comments the previous evening, was now totally confused as she turned to leave, both by the man and his suggestion that she occupy a bedroom in the main house. Not that it didn't have its appeal, because it did. The cottage was lonely as well as isolated; it reminded her how much she missed her mother, and Beth.

Though there had been times, Grace reflected ruefully, when she could have done with some personal space, if only to gather her thoughts together long enough to look beyond the daily drudge her life had become: taking care of her mother's needs in the morning, off to work for the lunchtime trade, and not back again until late in the evening, when she would be constantly on the alert in case her mother should need her during the night.

The last six months of her mother's life, when Grace had given up going to work completely, had been even more difficult, with never a single moment in the day or night that she could call her own.

Not that she in the least regretted or begrudged her mother that twenty-four-hour care—Heather and Clive had cared for and loved her since she was six weeks old, and it was no hardship for her to return that love and care. But it had meant that times of solitude, such as the hours she had spent alone in the cottage on this estate, had become a thing of the past.

'Oh, and Miss Blake?'

'Yes?' She turned slowly back to face her boss.

'I have invited two guests to dinner on Friday evening,

and I would appreciate it if you would organise and cook a special meal for the three of us.'

Grace all but gaped at him now. Oh, not because Cesar Navarro had asked her to cook the food for his dinner party in three days time—she could do that standing on her head, no matter how many guests he invited. No, it was the fact that he, a man reputed not to have a social or a private life, was having a dinner party at all that surprised her.

A fact she had all too clearly revealed if the derisive rise of his dark brows and mocking expression were any indication!

'Of course, Mr Navarro,' she agreed briskly, aiming for—but perhaps not reaching?—that discretion he had repeatedly remarked upon.

He nodded, that mockery still glinting in the darkness of his eyes as he sat back in the tall leather chair behind the desk. 'And, if possible, I would ask that you make the same delicious chocolate mousse from last night as the dessert. I have no doubts that one of my dinner guests, at least, would enjoy it very much.'

Grace was momentarily taken aback to see that the light in his eyes was now one of warmth rather than mockery. Because of thoughts of his dinner guest who would enjoy it very much if they could eat one of Grace's chocolate mousses? Her delicious chocolate mousses...

Grace had noted the empty and washed glass bowl on the draining board this morning when she entered the kitchen at six-thirty so that she could have Cesar's breakfast ready for seven o'clock, but she had assumed that Raphael, or Rodney, had been the one to empty the remains of the chocolate mousse into the bin before washing it; Cesar's comment now made her rethink that assumption. 'You obviously enjoyed it?' she prompted shrewdly.

'So much so that I believe its pleasurable qualities could almost be likened to those experienced during sex.'

'Whoa!' Grace took a step back to press against the panelled wall nearest the door.

'Did I say that out loud?' He eyed her mockingly.

Her cheeks burned. 'You know that you did!'

He arched a coolly mocking brow. 'You are allowed to say whatever outrageous comment comes into your head but I am not allowed to reciprocate?'

There was reciprocity, and then there was *reciprocity*—and Cesar Navarro had just stepped over the line into the latter.

Besides turning Grace's thoughts to imagining Cesar having sex, of all of that naked muscled leanness arched over a woman—over her!—as those firm and sensual lips kissed her breasts, and those long elegant hands caressed a path down from her breasts to her—

Oh, good grief!

For the second time in hours Grace found herself flushed and overheated with arousal. For Cesar Navarro!

A fact he was very well aware of if she read the mocking glint in those black eyes correctly.

A physical response Grace knew she was unable to deny as she felt her nipples once again spring to avid attention and press achingly against the lace of her bra, at the same time as that heat once again dampened her panties.

'Can it be that the outspoken Miss Blake has finally been rendered speechless?' he drawled.

Her eyes flashed her displeasure. 'I really don't think we should turn this into some sort of competition to see which one of us can shock the other the most!'

His expression was unreadable as he regarded her between those hooded lids. 'And are you shocked, Miss Blake?'

Was she? More than a twenty-six-year-old woman ought to be, if the truth were known—and where this man was concerned she seemed to be honest to the point of totally embarrassing herself!—especially a twenty-six-year-old woman who had spent a year living and working in a city as romantic as Paris.

She loved her job, enjoyed nothing more than creating beautifully cooked and presented food for others to enjoy. But cooking was so much more than that. It was an art. A delight for all the senses—as Cesar Navarro had obviously discovered when he ate the remains of her chocolate mousse the night before!—and it wasn't a skill that was easily acquired, or perfected overnight. Grace had studied for years, worked under several distinguished chefs, before even attempting to create dishes of her own, let alone the desserts and pastries in which she now specialised.

All of which had taken its toll on Grace's private life. Especially so when it came to having any sort of romantic relationship. A career as a chef meant working most lunch times and evenings, which didn't allow a lot of time for a social life, and Grace had learnt very early on that most men weren't willing to fit that social life around her career.

Which was one of the reasons Grace was still a virgin at the age of twenty-six.

Only one of them, of course. The other reason was more personal than that: a need inside her to find love, and permanence with a man, a special man, before she made love with him.

Maybe one of the reasons for that was the mystery surrounding her own birth and adoption. Beth had been luckier in some ways, in as much as she had always known her birth parents had been James and Carla Lawrence, both killed in a car accident when she was only five.

And wonderful adoptive parents as Clive and Heather

Blake had been to both of the little girls they had chosen as their own, Grace would be lying if she denied having given some thought, over the years, as to who her birth mother might have been. Whether or not she had been young and single, and unable to cope, either financially or emotionally, with a baby? Or if Grace had just been one child too many in a marriage already straining at the seams? Or if her mother might even have died in child-birth? The possible explanations for Grace being put up for adoption were endless.

Information was often available nowadays on the birth parents of adopted children, of course, and maybe one day Grace might decide to look into that; until two months ago, after Mum had died, it had somehow seemed disloyal to the wonderful couple who had adopted and raised her as their own to do so. But maybe one day Grace might see if she could find out who her birth mother had been. Find out if she was still alive. If she had any interest in meeting the woman her baby had become—

'If I had known it was going to take you this long to an-swer then I would not have asked the question!'

Grace gave a start as the impatience of Cesar's tone in-terrupted her personal meanderings, her smile rueful as she focused on him. 'No, I'm not in the least shocked by your remarks, Mr Navarro,' she assured him pertly.

'No?'

'No.' The hands clenching into fists at her sides im-mediately gave lie to that claim. How could she not be shocked—surprised—at the strange and intimate turn this conversation had taken?

Dark eyes glittered beneath hooded lids. 'In that case, I believe I mentioned having some work to do this morning?'

And, as Grace was quickly learning, a 'mention' from Cesar Navarro was as good as an order from anyone else!

'Of course.' She smiled coolly. 'Do you have any other dietary requests in regard to the dinner party on Friday evening?'

He gave the matter brief thought. 'I do not believe so, no…'

'Fine.' She nodded briskly. 'I'll put together a menu for your approval later today.'

'Along with your decision regarding moving into a bedroom in the east wing of the main house.'

'Along with my decision regarding moving into a bedroom in the east wing of the main house,' Grace echoed softly before finally leaving the study and closing the door firmly behind her, not at all sure it would be a good idea for her to move in here in the circumstances.

Those circumstances being her wholly physical—and unprecedented!—response to the 'gorgeously handsome' Cesar Navarro…

CHAPTER FOUR

'I SEE THAT YOU HAVE not only made your decision but already decided to move in— Careful, Miss Blake!' Cesar warned harshly even as he stepped further into the bedroom to reach out to grasp her arms to stop her from overbalancing as she stumbled slightly after turning sharply to face him.

'You know, you're either going to have to stop startling me in that way or run the risk of giving me a heart attack!' Her breasts quickly rose and fell as she trembled in his arms, her hands flat against the hardness of his chest. 'Difficult decision to make, hmm?' she added dryly as Cesar remained silent.

'You have no idea, Miss Blake!' Cesar grated as he straightened and released her abruptly, far too aware of the snug fit of the figure-hugging black jeans and the close fitting tee shirt Grace Blake wore, the latter clearly revealing the outline of the lace-cupped bra beneath, that long sable hair splayed out loosely over her shoulders. Hair that did indeed reach down to the pertness of her bottom in those figure-hugging jeans.

'You did not hurt your ankle when you stumbled?'

'Not in the least,' Grace reassured him lightly as she stepped away from him, knowing she was trembling slightly from his close proximity, the colour instantly warming her cheeks as she had the chance to take in his casual appearance.

'Have you been for a run…?' She knew her voice sounded slightly breathless as she found herself unable to look away from the width of Cesar's bared shoulders revealed by the sweat-dampened black vest-top he wore, with a pair of soft jogging bottoms, black this time, resting low on the leanness of his hips, the darkness of his hair damp and more tousled than usual, a black towel draped about his neck, the heat and purely masculine smell of his body seeming to wash over and overwhelm her in waves.

Slightly sweaty, his hair damp, he looked completely unlike his usual urbane—and haughtily remote—self, more earthy, and somehow primal…

Grace was still feeling slightly hot and bothered from being briefly held in his arms, and she now felt her own body respond to all that blatant maleness, her nipples once again tingling inside her bra, her jeans suddenly feeling tight and uncomfortable as she felt herself dampen and swell between her thighs. What was fast becoming her usual reaction to this man!

He gave a shake of his head. 'Raphael and I spent an hour or so sparring in the gym two floors above here. Ju jitsu,' he added dryly at Grace's enquiring glance.

'No doubt you're an expert, too.' Grace nodded ruefully.

'No doubt.' He nodded abruptly.

'Hmm. And to answer your question, yes, I thought I might take you up on your offer and give staying in the main house a try. See if I settle any better.' Although, if she was to keep seeing her boss dressed—or undressed!—in this way, she already knew exactly how it was going to go: a lot of physical squirming followed by as many cold showers!

'That is very magnanimous, of you, Miss Blake,' he drawled dryly.

Grace chose to ignore his obvious derision. 'Is it possible to have that switched off...?' She looked pointedly at the blinking camera in the corner of the bedroom. 'As I've already told you, I'm really not into exhibitionism,' she added with a grimace.

His mouth twisted ruefully. 'I will talk to Raphael.'

'Thank you.' Grace beamed her gratitude. 'Have you had a good day?' She hadn't been able to resist looking out of the window this morning when he had left the house, the attentive Raphael two steps behind him as usual, the other man opening the back door of the black SUV for his employer before taking his own seat in the front next to the chauffeur; now that Grace knew Raphael's true role, it was possible to see his tense watchfulness as he opened and closed the car door, and the way Rodney, standing guard beside the front door, treated Raphael with almost the same respect and deference he did Mr Navarro.

'It was tolerable,' Cesar found himself answering wryly. How many years had it been since anyone had asked him if he'd had a good day? His mother, perhaps, a dozen or so years ago, on the occasions when he'd returned to the home he had shared with her during the years he had spent at Harvard university.

He could not imagine anyone who affected him less maternally than Grace Blake, with her forthright manner and curvaceously arousing body!

A curvaceously arousing body he had been far too aware of—and aroused by!—as he held her in his arms a short time ago... 'And your own day?' he prompted tersely.

She shrugged narrow shoulders. 'I managed to keep busy.'

Cesar gave an exasperated shake of his head. 'I do not

understand why you applied for this job in the first place when you are obviously too highly qualified for such a position.'

She arched her brows. 'Honestly?'

He grimaced. 'Why bother to change the tenor of our acquaintance at this late date?'

She smiled slightly. 'I tried but wasn't able to get a job in a hotel or restaurant after my eight months…sabbatical, and my sister, Beth, doesn't earn near enough to support us both and pay off all the debts that accumulated when— I needed the money,' she repeated uncomfortably.

And thanks to Maddox's file on her, Cesar knew that it was her mother's protracted illness, and eventual death two months ago, that had resulted in Grace accumulating those debts she had almost spoken of.

'I thought your sister's name was Elizabeth?'

'How did you—? The security check.' Grace grimaced in acknowledgement. 'Then you also know the reason I took that sabbatical. We've always called my sister Beth, not Elizabeth,' she amended with a pained frown.

'I am sorry for your loss.' Cesar had had chance to read all of Grace's file now—in fact he had made a point of it!—and knew that her adoptive father had also died four years ago, the only family she had left being her also adopted sister, Elizabeth.

'Beth and I still have each other.' Grace shrugged philosophically. 'We often drove each other insane when we were both in our teens,' she recalled ruefully, 'but we're very close now. But you have a younger sister of your own, so you probably know how annoying that can be when you're growing up,' she dismissed wryly, only to give a pained frown as she easily saw the change that had come over Cesar Nevarro; every muscle in that magnificent body seemed to have tensed, a nerve pulsing in the firmness of his jaw, those black eyes glittering in warning.

Why? Because she had admitted to knowing something of his own family?

She gave a rueful grimace. 'It seemed only fair that I should do a little security check on you, too!'

'Then the source of that security check was obviously not up to date,' he dismissed stiffly.

'Sorry…?'

'My sister's name was Gabriela, Miss Blake, and we lost her when she was two years old,' he bit out abruptly. 'Now, if you will excuse me—'

'Oh, no,' Grace groaned in contrition as she quickly crossed the room to his side. 'I'm so sorry.' She reached out and placed a hand on the tenseness of his lower arm, before as quickly removing it, her eyes widening, as she felt the equivalent of an electric shock enter her fingers and tingle up her arm. 'That was so insensitive— I had no idea…' She thrust that still-tingling hand behind her back, her cheeks slightly flushed.

He looked down the long length of his nose at her. 'Obviously.'

Oh, ground, just open up and swallow her now, Grace inwardly pleaded, anything to escape the disdain in those cold and glittering eyes.

'I suggest that in future if you wish to know anything about my private life, that you ask me for that information, and not jump to inaccurate conclusions or look it up on unreliable websites,' he advised coldly.

She nodded. 'I really am so very sorry.'

She looked so earnest in her contrition that Cesar felt some of his own tension easing a little. But only a little. The subject of his sister, Gabriela, was still a sensitive one, and not something that his parents, or any of their family acquaintances, ever spoke of in his presence.

He had been ten years older than Gabriela, but he had adored his blonde-haired and impishly mischievous little sister from the day she was born, her loss an emotional trauma from which none of his family had ever truly recovered. His parents' marriage hadn't survived the loss, the two of them remaining together only until Cesar reached the age of eighteen, when his mother had returned to America, and his father had continued living in Argentina. They had never divorced each other, and to his knowledge neither of them had ever had anyone else in their lives; it was just too painful for them to live together with Gabriela's little ghost standing between them.

He drew in a harsh breath as he stepped away from Grace. 'If you will excuse me? I need to shower and change before dinner.'

'Of course.' Her face was very pale, her eyes appearing huge in that pallor.

Cesar relented slightly at her obvious distress. 'The bowl of fruit you have placed in the entrance hall is a vast improvement on the flowers.'

'Well, if you think so…' She looked unconvinced. 'Er— you mentioned the east wing— Is it okay for me to use this bedroom?'

'Is it not a little late to ask me that when you have obviously already moved all of your things in here?' There were clothes hanging up in the open wardrobe, books piled high on the bedside table, an open and half-emptied suitcase on the bed.

'I was attempting to be polite.'

'As I said earlier, that is perhaps a little too late?' He quirked a dark brow.

Embarrassed colour now brightened her cheeks. 'I have

no idea why but I just keep blurting my thoughts out loud every time I speak with you!'

Cesar had no idea, either, why it was he tolerated Miss Blake's outspokenness.

Perhaps it was as he had thought, because for the most part he found her candour amusing, even refreshing, after years of having his instructions carried out without question?

Most of the time.

The shock of hearing her speak of Gabriela, the sister who was for ever lost to him, had not been in the least amusing.

'Perhaps in future you should try harder,' he bit out tersely.

'Yes.' She gave an awkward grimace.

He nodded tersely. 'I will leave you to finish your unpacking.'

Grace looked down frowningly at her still-tingling hand, before glancing up to watch Cesar Navarro as he moved down the hallway with the elegant grace of a predator, in the direction of the west wing, where she knew his own suite of rooms was situated.

Huge palatial rooms that Kevin had instructed her to make ready for Cesar's arrival yesterday, the sitting-room elegantly furnished, the bathroom the height of luxury with its sunken bath and separate glass shower unit, the bedroom dominated by a huge four-poster bed.

A four-poster bed in which it was now all too easy for Grace to imagine that lean and muscled body nakedly reclining, his tousled hair dark against the cream pillows...

She clenched her tingling hand into a fist before turning back into the much smaller guest bedroom she had chosen for herself, knowing she had well and truly put her size four feet in it when she had unknowingly talked of Cesar's sister.

There had been absolutely no mention of his sister's death on the website she had looked at before coming here. Probably because, as Cesar had told her yesterday, he owned or had influence over much of today's media, and the subject of his sister's death was no more something he wished to be on a public website than the details of his own personal life?

Whatever the reason, Grace knew that by bringing up the subject of Gabriela she had succeeded in irritating him all over again.

At this rate she really was going to find herself unemployed again before the end of the week!

Which might not be a bad thing, considering her completely physical response just now to touching Cesar Navarro…

'Mr Navarro has asked that you go through to the dining-room,' Raphael informed Grace later that evening as she finished preparing a tray of coffee.

Aware now of Raphael's role as head of Cesar's security, Grace had done her best to break the ice between them this evening, ignoring what appeared to be his habitual taciturn nature as she chatted to him lightly between serving the courses. Just general chit-chat, to which she had usually only received acknowledging grunts rather than any real conversation back, but Raphael did seem a little less frosty than he had yesterday.

'I'll take the tray of coffee through with me, shall I?' Grace offered lightly.

'If you wish.' He gave an abrupt inclination of his head as he stepped back.

'Don't look so worried, Raphael.' Her eyes danced with

laughter as she moved to pick up the silver tray. 'As I've already assured Mr Navarro, I have absolutely no intention of adding poison to his coffee!'

Raphael's expression remained stern. 'You find Mr Navarro's security a subject for amusement?'

'Well, no, of course not,' she conceded a little guiltily. 'But is all this cloak and dagger stuff really necessary?'

He arched one brow. 'Cloak and dagger?'

Grace smiled slightly at how much like his arrogant employer Raphael looked at that moment.

'People, real people, don't actually live like this, you know. Guards everywhere, security cameras in the grounds and most of the rooms, movement sensors in the ones that don't,' she elaborated as Raphael continued to look down at her blankly.

'You are suggesting that Cesar is not a real person?'

'Of course not, I just—' She gave an uncomfortable shake of her head. 'I just find it all a little over the top.'

There was a slight softening about the stern set of Raphael's mouth. 'I realise that, to outsiders, this level of security might seem extreme.'

'And I'm definitely an outsider,' Grace muttered ruefully.

'Perhaps if you were aware—' Raphael broke off abruptly. 'People in Cesar's position are vulnerable to any number of dangers.'

'People as wealthy as him, you mean?'

'If you will, yes,' Raphael confirmed flatly.

'And to think, I never realised before that there were advantages to being poor!' she came back ruefully.

Raphael gave a brief wince of exasperation. 'Cesar warned me that you can be…somewhat unusual, in some of your comments.'

Grace gave a shrug. 'So you think all of this is necessary?' Did Cesar Navarro really need to have a personal bodyguard, namely Raphael, accompany him everywhere? For his place of residence—whichever of his homes around the world that might be!—to be kept constantly under surveillance, by cameras as well as numerous security guards?

'Family history would imply so, yes,' Raphael answered unhelpfully. 'Mr Navarro is still waiting,' he reminded, giving the vaguest of smiles as he pointedly opened the kitchen door for her.

'Thanks,' Grace accepted dryly as she swept jauntily out of the room with the laden tray; heaven forbid Mr Navarro should be kept waiting.

Although that jauntiness faded as Grace made her way through the house to the dining-room, as she wondered what family history Raphael could be referring to.

Only for those thoughts to fade the nearer she got to the dining-room, butterflies fluttering in her stomach as she remembered her completely physical response earlier to just touching Cesar Navarro's arm, her hand having continued to tingle long after he had left her bedroom.

After he had left her bedroom...

Maybe moving into the main house hadn't been such a good idea, after all?

It really was too late to be pondering the wisdom of that now, when she had already moved in.

Besides which, Cesar was way, way out of her league. He inhabited a different world from her. Financially, socially, physically.

Oh, most definitely physically...

It seemed ludicrous to her now to think she had ever believed Cesar Navarro and Raphael might be a couple; her boss might be remote, even coldly disciplined, but there had been a definite physical appreciation in the darkness of his hooded gaze earlier as he stood in the doorway to her bedroom looking so virile and male, in the black vest top and black jogging trousers, the darkness of his hair tousled from his exertions in the gym.

Dark and tousled hair Grace's fingers had ached to touch!

And a maleness that made her legs weak!

'Please come in, Miss Blake,' he said in answer to her knock on the dining-room door. 'Was the knock because you expected me to be dancing around the room naked?' he prompted dryly as Grace pushed open the door and entered the room.

'Not with the security cameras in here, no,' she came back pertly, her gaze avoiding that mocking dark one as she crossed the dining-room and placed the tray down on the table in front of him.

But not before Grace had a chance to take in his appearance, in a loose white silk shirt that emphasised the width of those muscled shoulders and the leanness of his abdomen, several buttons undone at his throat, revealing the start of that silky dark hair on his chest.

She straightened abruptly. 'Raphael said you wanted to talk to me?'

Cesar observed Grace between narrowed lids as he saw her own lids were lowered—in order to avoid meeting his gaze?—and so allowing him opportunity to take in her appearance in another formal white blouse and black skirt, the long length of her hair once again secured at her crown; a stark contrast to those tight jeans and that fitted tee shirt she had been wearing earlier, with that long sable-coloured hair allowed to flow loosely down the length of her slender spine.

He straightened in his chair. 'Sit down, Miss Blake.'

Her surprised gaze flicked up to his and then down

again. 'That really wouldn't be appropriate to employer-employee relations, Mr Navarro.'

His mouth tightened. 'I am that employer, Miss Blake, and I have asked that you sit.'

'Not to be nitpicking, but I believe you told rather than—'

'*Madre mia!* Sit down, Miss Blake!' he thundered in exasperation.

'Okay, okay,' she acquiesced hastily as she obviously heard that impatience in his tone, moving to the other end of the table before pulling out the chair and perching on the edge of it. 'Raphael wouldn't approve, you know,' she muttered.

'I do not recall asking for Raphael's approval.' Cesar looked down the length of the table at her.

Grace was uncomfortably aware of the fact that she and Cesar Navarro were alone in the dining room. Except they weren't, not really—because those intrusive security cameras were even now recording their every move!

'As I have no intention of shouting down the table at you I suggest you move a little closer,' he advised impatiently.

A frown creased Grace's brow. 'Was there something wrong with your dinner? Because, if so—'

'As I am sure you are well aware, my meal this evening was, as last night, excellent,' Cesar drawled dismissively. 'I just have no intention of raising my voice in order to be heard,' he added pointedly.

'Oh.' She got up to move awkwardly back down the length of the table before sitting gingerly on the chair to the left of where he sat at the head of the table. 'Do you enjoy eating alone?'

Cesar blinked. 'It is not a matter of enjoyment or otherwise; I live alone so I eat alone.'

'But you could have invited any number of—' She broke off with a wince.

'Those hordes of beautiful woman I take to my silk-sheeted bed every night to join me?'

The colour brightened her cheeks. 'Yes.'

'She is back, I see.' Cesar smiled tightly.

Grace Blake blinked. '"She"?'

'The outspoken Miss Blake,' he drawled dryly as he relaxed back in his chair to regard her with mocking dark eyes.

Grace gave a rueful grimace, her shoulders slumping slightly. 'And I was really trying this time, too!'

'Then, again, you obviously failed.' He shrugged.

It was becoming something of an occupational hazard where this man was concerned, Grace acknowledged heavily.

'Do you approve of the menu for Friday evening?' She changed the subject as she saw the menu she had written out for him, and sent up with Raphael earlier, lying on the table beside Cesar Navarro's place setting.

'I am sure my two guests will thoroughly enjoy it.' He nodded.

'And you?'

He gave a haughty inclination of his head. 'And me.'

Especially the sexy chocolate mousse?

The thought came unbidden into Grace's head. And just as quickly she wished that it hadn't. Imagining Cesar Navarro in the throes of orgasmic bliss was really not a good idea!

'Was that all?'

'Would you care to join me for coffee?'

Grace's eyes widened at the unexpected invitation. 'I only brought one cup.'

'Then perhaps a glass of brandy?' He indicated the decanter and glasses on the side dresser.

She gave another grimace. 'I tend to get even more outspoken if I drink alcohol.' And, as this man had already observed—on more than one occasion!—she was already verbose enough in his company, without a glass of brandy to loosen her tongue even further!

'I believe I am willing to take the risk if you are, Miss Blake?' There was no missing the amusement in Cesar's tone.

And Grace had never been one to back down from a challenge.

'In that case, thank you,' she accepted stiffly.

He rose and crossed the room to pour brandy into two of the crystal glasses, shoulders wide and waist lean beneath the white silk shirt, tailored black trousers sitting loosely on his hips as he again moved with all the silent grace of a predator.

Because he was a predator, of the sharp-toothed variety, Grace reminded herself as she carefully avoided so much as touching his fingers as she took the glass of brandy from him, too aware of her earlier reaction to lightly touching his arm to want a repeat of that skin-tingling experience.

He resumed his seat at the head of the table, the darkness of his gaze easily holding hers over the rim of his glass as he took a sip of his own drink before speaking.

'You do not appear to be drinking, Miss Blake.'

Grace gave a pained frown. 'That's probably because I'm a little…uncertain of why I'm here?'

'At this precise moment you are being invited to enjoy a glass of brandy,' he drawled with a pointed glance towards her untouched glass of the deep amber liquid.

She moistened her lips, and instantly wished she hadn't as those lips instantly became the focus of that dark and hawkish gaze. Her cheeks warmed under the intensity of those piercing dark eyes, her hand trembling slightly as she reached out to pick up the beautiful crystal glass before taking a tentative sip of the contents. 'Excellent,' she murmured appreciatively. 'But then, it would be, wouldn't it?' She shrugged. 'Only the best for Cesar Navarro,' she explained ruefully as he arched a questioning brow.

His mouth thinned. 'And you do not approve?'

'It's not for me to approve or disapprove of anything you do.' Grace avoided looking at him as she placed the glass carefully back on the place mat so as not to mark the oak dining table.

'I assure you, that has not been my experience so far,' he replied dryly.

The heat intensified in Grace's cheeks. 'I did warn you what happens when I drink alcohol.'

'So you did,' he conceded. 'Tell me, have you ever considered the idea of opening your own restaurant?'

'Sorry?' She was taken aback at the sudden change of subject.

Cesar slowly sipped his brandy before repeating the question. 'I asked if you have ever thought of opening your own restaurant.'

Only every day since Grace reached the age of sixteen and knew she wanted to become the best chef in England!

It was a pipe dream, of course. Oh, she had gone to Paris to study under a master chef, worked in several hotels there once she had completed her training, before moving back to England to become the pastry chef in one of the leading hotels in London. But the dream of one day opening her own restaurant was still just that, and always would be.

She gave a rueful shake of her head. 'That takes capital I simply don't have, Mr Navarro.'

'I understood that you owned half of your parents' house in London?'

That damned security check again! Was there anything this man didn't know about her?

'And my sister owns the other half. A house we both live in,' she added pointedly. 'Talking of which… Would it be okay for Beth to come down here and stay with me one weekend?'

Cesar smiled tightly. 'I was not aware that you needed my permission to invite your sister to visit you?'

She grimaced. 'But I do need you to okay the visit with Raphael in order for the security guards to allow Beth through the gates.'

Cesar stood up impatiently. 'No matter what you may think to the contrary, Miss Blake, you are not a prisoner here.'

'Does that mean I can invite Beth?'

'Of course you may invite—' Cesar broke off, a nerve pulsing in his tightly clenched jaw as he drew in a deep, controlling breath. He never raised his voice in anger. Had never needed to. Before the annoying Grace Blake entered his life, that was. 'As long as you inform Raphael first, you may invite any visitor here that you wish.'

She shook her head. 'There's only Beth.'

He arched dark brows. 'No man to share your own silk-sheeted bed?'

'My bed doesn't have silk sheets.' Her cheeks blazed a fiery red. 'Nor, if it did, is there a man in my life to share it with.'

'Currently?'

She frowned. 'Ever!'

He frowned slightly. 'Are you being coy, Miss Blake?'

'I'm saying, as politely as possible, that my private life

is none of your damned business.' Anger now underlined her tone. 'Now, can my sister visit one weekend or not?'

Cesar gave a cool inclination of his head. 'I have said that she may. Not this weekend, of course, because we will not be back until Sunday. But—'

'Back?' She looked up at him blankly. 'Back from where?'

Cesar realised from the blankness of the expression on Grace Blake's face that he had somehow omitted to tell her where his dinner party was to take place on Friday evening. The dinner party she would be catering...

CHAPTER FIVE

Buenos Aires!

UNBELIEVABLE AS IT still seemed to Grace, she found herself seated in Cesar Navarro's private jet late on Thursday
night, on her way to his home in the Argentinian capital,
for the sole purpose of cooking a meal for him and the two
guests he had informed her would be with him for dinner
tomorrow evening.

People actually did things like this! Well...it seemed
that Cesar Navarro actually did things like this.

It had taken the rest of that glass of brandy for Grace
to recover from the shock of learning she was expected to
go Buenos Aires with him for the weekend.

Grace had immediately telephoned Beth to ask if she
could courier her passport down to her, Beth no more
happy than Grace once she had explained why she needed
that passport, her sister agreeing to courier over the passport at the same time as she questioned the wisdom of
Grace going to Argentina for the weekend with a man she
had only just met, even if he was her employer.

Grace thought of confiding in Beth as to her own res-
ervations, only to as quickly dismiss the idea; having only
just met the man, Grace felt it best not to admit to Beth just
how disturbed she was at the prospect of going away for

the weekend to a city reputed to be as throbbing with excitement as Buenos Aires—with a man who clearly made her throb with excitement!

She glanced across at him now as he and Raphael talked softly together as they sat in two of the armchairs across from her own in the luxurious cabin of the private jet, six comfortable chairs in all, the rest of the space given over to two sofas, several tables, and a wide-screened television. There was also a fully equipped galley, from where the steward had served them with a meal worthy of any of the restaurants or hotels Grace had worked in the last four years, and where her fresh ingredients for tomorrow night's dinner had been stored in one of the huge refrigerators.

Cesar had informed her that it was early spring in Argentina at the moment, and advised that Grace dress warmly, which she had done, by wearing jeans and a jumper.

Nevertheless, she had been unprepared for Cesar's own casual appearance in a loose black shirt unbuttoned at his throat and worn beneath a black leather jacket, faded denims that fitted low on the leanness of his hips, and heavy black boots. And if that wasn't enough to set her pulse racing, there was always the overlong darkness of his hair in that usual tousled style, that made Grace long to thread her fingers through it and see if it really was as silky soft as it looked.

So not what Grace should be thinking about when she was on her way to spend two nights in Cesar Navarro's Buenos Aires apartment with him.

Not alone, of course. The ever-watchful Raphael would be with them. And no doubt several security guards. But even so...

As if sensing her gaze on him, Cesar broke off his conversation with Raphael to look across at her enquiringly, one dark brow rising as Grace immediately felt the warmth of colour in her cheeks at being caught ogling him so blatantly. Her colour deepened as he murmured softly to Raphael before standing up to cross the cabin and lower his lean length into the chair opposite Grace's, all the time looking at her with those enigmatic black eyes, and exuding that aura of raw power that no doubt made him a formidable businessman.

And even more formidable as a man!

'You are nervous of flying?' he prompted softly.

'Not at all,' Grace dismissed stiffly.

He nodded. 'Once again you seem a little discomforted by your surroundings?'

'Overwhelmed, actually,' she admitted huskily.

'It is just a jet, Grace,' he dismissed as he stretched those long legs out in front of him.

'Just a private jet that the pilot flies wherever you tell him to,' she corrected, inwardly knowing that this man overwhelmed her more than her surroundings. Maybe she should have confided in Beth, as to her confusion of feelings for this man, after all? Beth had a far more practical way of looking at things than Grace did.

As it was, Cesar seemed different tonight, somehow bigger, more immediate in the confines of this luxurious cabin and dressed in those casual clothes. A physical force to be reckoned with. A physical force that Grace knew she was having more and more difficulty ignoring.

It was…unsettling.

Cesar Navarro was unsettling.

The way he looked tonight. The way he smelt—an expensive cologne, along with that earthy warmth that was purely Cesar. The fact that he appeared to be in control of all that he surveyed.

Probably because he was in control of all he surveyed—

including her, Grace acknowledged. She felt wrong-footed and out of her depth sitting beside him in the luxury of his private jet, so much so that she couldn't think of a single one of those pithy comebacks that had become such a part of their relationship.

They didn't have a relationship, Grace reminded herself firmly, except for that of employer and employee.

'There is a bedroom at the back of the plane if you would care to rest for a few hours?'

Grace's eyes widened. A bedroom? There was a bed on board this plane?

Well, of course there was a bed on the plane, she instantly chided herself; Cesar Navarro flew all over the world on this jet, no doubt often crossing several time zones in the process, and he would need to be able to sleep during those long flights in order to be rested for the business meetings he attended once he arrived at his destination.

She moistened the fullness of her lips before answering him huskily. 'I couldn't possibly think of depriving you of your rest.'

He eyed her laughingly. 'It is a very large bed.'

Her eyes widened. Surely he couldn't mean— He wasn't suggesting—? 'Really, I'm fine here.' Her cheeks were flushed a bright and revealing red as she gave Raphael a self-conscious glance beneath her lashes.

Cesar also glanced across at his Head of Security, the other man having laid his head back against the chair, his eyes closed as if in sleep. A politeness, of course, to give the impression of allowing a degree of privacy between Cesar and Grace; in all the years Raphael had worked for him, Cesar had never known the other man to fall asleep during one of these long flights. He wasn't sure the ever-watchful man ever slept!

Cesar's hooded gaze turned to the red-faced Grace. 'It is a long flight.'

'Nevertheless—'

Cesar gave an exasperated sigh. 'Do you have to argue about everything, Miss Blake?'

She looked back at him curiously. 'Do you do that deliberately?'

He frowned. 'Do what deliberately?'

'Constantly address me as Miss Blake.'

'It is your name.' His jaw tightened. 'And you have not given me permission to call you anything else.'

She raised mocking brows. 'Do you need my permission?'

'I believe so, yes.'

'That's a very old-fashioned attitude.'

Cesar eyed her impatiently. 'Or merely an Argentinian courtesy.'

'Then please call me Grace,' she invited dryly. 'And to answer your question, I didn't argue when you told me we were coming to Buenos Aires for the weekend, did I?'

'Only because you were too surprised at the time to do so. Speechless, in fact. It was a most refreshing change,' he added with satisfaction.

An irritated frown creased her creamy brow. 'Not everyone is used to jumping on their private jet and flying thousands of miles around the world just for a dinner party!'

'But it is not just any dinner party,' Cesar drawled ruefully.

She stilled. 'You should have told me if it's a special occasion.'

'Why?'

'I might have chosen a different menu.'

'The menu is fine as it is. And I do not find reaching the age of thirty-four a reason for celebration.' He grimaced.

She gasped. 'It's your birthday?'

Cesar glanced down at the expensive watch on his wrist. 'It would appear so, yes.'

Grace could only stare at him, knowing she really was at a loss for words this time. She was flying to Cesar Navarro's apartment in Buenos Aires to cook dinner for his birthday party? Well, not a birthday party as such, as there would only be two guests beside himself. Now that she knew it was his birthday, Grace couldn't help wondering exactly who those other two guests might be. Especially the one who would very much enjoy her chocolate mousse.

Perhaps the same woman currently sharing his silk-sheeted bed? In Buenos Aires, at least.

Grace's heart sank just imagining being in the same apartment when Cesar shared his bed with another woman.

Oh, dear Lord, where had that thought come from?

She couldn't be seriously attracted to a man as out of her league as Cesar Navarro? It would be madness on her part. Utter madness, that could—would—only lead to heartbreak.

She gave a firm shake of her head, as much for her own benefit as Cesar's. 'I had no idea. You really should have told me it was your birthday.'

'Would you have baked a cake?' he asked. 'Or perhaps bought me a gift?'

'Yes, to the cake,' Grace answered distractedly. 'But what could I possibly buy for the man who already has everything?' she added tartly.

His mouth thinned. 'There are many things in life I do not have, Grace.'

'Such as?'

He shrugged. 'Such as two parents who still live together, something my own parents have been unable to do happily since we lost Gabriela.'

She gave a soft gasp, her eyes going dark with compassion. 'Is that the reason your parents separated?'

'Eventually, yes.' A nerve pulsed in his tightly clenched jaw. 'Some families are drawn closer together in such situations, I believe. Others, like my own parents, cannot bear the loss that consumes them every time they look at each other—and I have absolutely no idea why I am telling you any of this!' He stared at her in exasperation.

'Maybe because, after all this time, you felt the need to talk to someone about it?'

His nostrils flared. 'That does not explain why I would choose to talk to you.'

Grace drew back sharply. 'That was incredibly rude.'

Was Cesar's annoyance with himself because she was only an employee? Or was it solely because her boss was a very private man, who never discussed his private life with anyone?

'I apologise,' he muttered stiffly, staring at her between narrowed lids for several long seconds before standing up abruptly. 'If you should change your mind, and wish to rest, the bedroom is through the door at the back of the cabin.' He strode back to sit in his chair beside Raphael before resting his own head back, closing his eyes and eventually seeming to fall asleep, his expression remaining harshly unforgiving.

It was a sleep that totally eluded Grace. Firstly, because of the tears she felt like shedding because of Cesar's hurtful rejection of her sympathetic ear. Secondly, because she couldn't stop thinking about the things Cesar had just told her about his parents. Being adopted, wondering who her real parents might have been, had always been painful enough, but Grace simply couldn't imagine—didn't want to imagine!—how heartbreaking it must have been to lose the two-year-old daughter the Navarro family had all so obviously adored.

'This is amazing...'

Cesar glanced at the woman seated beside him in the back of the air-conditioned limousine that had been waiting at the airport to drive them into Buenos Aires, Raphael seated in the glass-partitioned front of the car beside the driver, the other man's expression unreadable behind dark glasses as he kept a constant watch on their surroundings.

Cesar had spent much of the flight here regretting both his conversation with Grace Blake, in regard to his parents, and the tears he had seen in those blue-green eyes when he had brought an abrupt—and, yes, he admitted it, rude—end to that conversation. He never discussed his family with anyone, family or friends, and Grace Blake was neither of those things. Which made his conversation with her all the more bizarre.

His expression softened now as he saw her enthralled expression as she gazed out of the smoked-glass window beside her at the sights and sounds of Buenos Aires. 'I take it you have never been to Argentina before?'

She gave a shake of her head, the smoothness of her long sable hair cascading silkily down the length of her spine. 'My parents were both lawyers, and so we could afford to go to places like Florida and the Caribbean for holidays when Beth and I were younger. But we never came to Argentina. I have been to the musical, though, and seen the film, and even have the tee shirt!' she added ruefully.

Cesar looked at her quizzically. 'I do not— Ah.' He nodded. 'That was the Argentina of fifty years ago. It has become somewhat more cosmopolitan since then.'

'It's wonderful!' Her eyes glowed. 'I love the way the

new buildings, and even the colourful graffiti, complement rather than detract from the older architecture. And the people look so relaxed sitting outside in cafés and restaurants, and I'm sure I saw a crowd watching a couple dance in the street a few minutes ago—'

'The tango.' Cesar nodded. 'It is often performed in many of our streets and squares by roving musicians and dancers, and the crowd is encouraged to join in.'

Grace's eyes widened. 'Have you ever—? No, of course you haven't.' She blushed.

Cesar's mouth twitched. 'I have never performed the tango in public, no, but no self-respecting Argentinian man could call himself such if he could not at least dance the tango.'

'Oh.' She looked nonplussed.

He arched a brow. 'And do you also dance the tango?'

'Badly.' She smiled ruefully. 'My parents were really into ballroom dancing, and insisted that Beth and I take lessons in our teens.'

'My parents, also.' He nodded.

'Beth is much better at it than me,' Grace added affectionately. 'She has a natural rhythm.'

'And you do not?'

The huskiness of Cesar's voice made Grace wonder if they were still talking about dancing the tango?

'I get by.' Her gaze dropped from meeting the intensity of that black one as she answered him, her palms becoming slightly damp as she imagined performing that erotic dance with Cesar Navarro, the lean length of his body against hers as they performed the complicated steps, gazing into each other's eyes as they—

Never going to happen, Grace, she told herself firmly. She was only here to cook, for Cesar's birthday dinner, no less, not become heated at the thought of performing the tango with him.

She shifted uncomfortably on the leather seat. 'Do we have much further to go to your apartment? I would really like to freshen up after that long journey.' After her thoughts of a few minutes ago, a cold shower seemed like a good idea!

'Another few minutes, that is all.' He shrugged dismissively before glancing out of the window beside him.

Giving Grace the opportunity to look at him unobserved. He had removed his jacket and turned back the cuffs of his shirt to just below his elbows before getting into the back of the car with her, revealing the muscled length of his lower arms covered in a fine dusting of dark hair, that plain gold watch strapped about his left wrist, his hands wide as they rested on his muscled thighs, his fingers long and graceful, and leading Grace to wonder how those hands would feel—

This had to stop.

Before she made a complete fool of herself!

'You were expecting something else…?' Cesar saw the surprise on Grace Blake's face as she got slowly out of the car onto the cobbled courtyard of his home in the Recoleta area of Buenos Aires, Raphael busy organising the removal of their luggage from the boot of the car by several of his security team.

'But I thought you said you lived in an apartment?'

'The top floor of this building, yes. You were expecting a modern high rise like the ones in your English cities, perhaps?' Cesar guessed.

Whatever Grace had been expecting it wasn't this beautiful four-storey mansion house overlooking spacious parkland and gardens, where she could see families picnicking, children playing, and assorted dogs being walked on leads. 'I had no idea…' she murmured softly.

Cesar nodded. 'The area of Recoleta is considered an oasis of peace in an otherwise teeming city.'

A very exclusive—very wealthy—area in an otherwise teeming city, Grace guessed ruefully as she slowly followed Cesar into the coolness of the building, their footsteps sounding loud as they crossed the marble entrance hall to the lifts. Three of them. No doubt a private one for each floor of the building.

'No Raphael?' Grace quirked a brow as Cesar stood to one side waiting for her to enter the lift once the doors had glided noiselessly open, finding she was becoming more aware of when the other man wasn't around now than when he was.

'He will join us once he has dealt with the luggage,' Cesar replied as he stepped into the large and mirrored lift beside her.

She really had entered another world when she accepted this job as Cesar Navarro's cook/housekeeper, Grace acknowledged dazedly. An exclusive world of extensive English estates, private jets, chauffeur-driven limousines, exclusive Buenos Aires apartments—and the inevitable security cameras, she realised as she glanced up ruefully at the one in the corner of the lift.

Cesar's mouth tightened as he saw the direction of Grace Blake's gaze. 'Why do they bother you so much?' he prompted impatiently as he pressed the button for the lift to ascend.

She turned to look at him. 'Why don't they bother you at all?'

He raised one dark brow. 'Why should they?'

'Because—well, because they take away any chance of privacy!'

'And what privacy could you possibly require in a lift?'

'I—well—I don't know! It's just— What are you doing?' she demanded breathlessly as Cesar turned and placed his hands on the mirrored wall of the lift either side of her head as he looked down at her, the length of his body only inches away from her own as she felt herself tremble at that close proximity.

'I am endeavouring to demonstrate that my own movements are not in the least inhibited by the presence of those cameras.' Cesar breathed shallowly as he looked down at her between narrowed lids, his gaze moving slowly from her wide blue-green eyes, down to those endearing freckles across her nose, to the fullness of her pouting lips.

A pouting mouth that Cesar freely acknowledged he had found himself thinking of far too often these past four days, as he wondered if they would taste as soft and delicious as they looked.

Parted and pouting lips, which Grace now moistened nervously with the tip of her little pink tongue before speaking huskily. 'Cesar?'

The warmth of her breath was a light caress against his own lips as he angled and lowered his head so that only centimetres now separated them. 'Yes?'

She shifted uncomfortably. 'I believe you've more than proven your point.'

Cesar continued to look down at her for several long, tense seconds as his usual reserve warred with the increasing need he felt to taste the fullness of Grace Blake's mouth.

She was his employee, damn it, and a young woman who had simply accompanied her employer to Buenos Aires for the sole purpose of cooking and serving dinner this evening. A beautiful and desirable young woman, but Cesar's employee, nonetheless.

'So I have,' he rasped, his jaw tight as he pushed away from the wall to step back as the lift came to a halt and the doors opened to allow them to step out into the cool entrance hall of his apartment.

Grace followed him slowly on legs that felt decidedly shaky, sure that she must have been mistaken about that brief flare of hunger she thought she'd seen in Cesar Navarro's jet-black eyes a few seconds ago as he looked down at her mouth; it was more likely to have been displeasure rather than hunger.

As his standing so close to her at all had been a punishment for her criticism, and designed to show her that he really wasn't in the least bothered by those cameras.

'*Bon dia*, Maria,' Cesar warmly greeted the tiny, grey-haired woman dressed in black who had appeared in the entrance hall.

An entrance hall and apartment that were every bit as opulent as the nineteenth-century architecture outside had indicated it might be: Moorish mosaics on the floors, intricately painted ceilings, along with French cornices decorated in rich gold, and beautiful chandeliers hanging from those arched ceilings, the antique furniture of dark wood, with several low and comfortable-looking sofas.

Grace had absolutely no idea what the elderly woman had said in reply to Cesar's greeting, but her smile and the pleasure glowing in the darkness of her eyes clearly showed her warmth of regard for her employer.

'Maria, this is Miss Grace Blake. My housekeeper, Maria Sanchez.' Cesar was still smiling as he turned to make the introductions. 'No,' he said stiffly as the housekeeper asked a question, adding something else dismissively in Spanish.

Grace looked at him enquiringly even as she shook hands with the older woman.

His mouth twisted derisively. 'Maria enquired if you would be sharing my bedroom suite. Obviously I have assured her you will not,' he added dryly as Grace blushed her discomfort.

He had said a lot more than that, Grace knew, no doubt informing the older woman that, like Maria, she was just another employee.

No, not even like the smiling Maria, Grace acknowledged ruefully; Cesar treated the elderly woman with obvious affection, whereas she seemed to irritate him more often than not.

'I can easily make up a bed for myself in one of the bedrooms if that would be less trouble for Maria,' Grace offered huskily.

'That will not be necessary. The guests suites are always prepared and available for use.' Cesar turned to say something else to his housekeeper in Spanish before turning back to Grace. 'I have some work to do now, but Maria will take you to the green guest suite and then show you to the kitchen. Raphael will arrive shortly with your luggage and the things you need to prepare for this evening's meal.'

'What time would you like to eat dinner?'

He frowned slightly. 'My guests will arrive about eight-thirty, so nine o'clock, if that suits you?'

'That's fine.'

'It has been a long night, and as this evening will also be late, I suggest you take advantage of a siesta this afternoon.' He nodded to Grace dismissively before turning on his heel and striding down the hallway to the right of the entrance hall.

Grace's legs still felt slightly shaky from that incident in the lift as she followed Maria down the hallway to the green suite, so much so that she wasn't even overwhelmed this time by the opulence of the bedroom overlooking the park, or the luxurious cream and gold bathroom adjoining it, which Maria informed her in halting English was her own private bathroom.

What would she have done if Cesar had actually carried out his unspoken threat and kissed her?

She would have kissed him right back, came the unequivocal answer.

And no doubt enjoyed every moment of it...

Where was the practical Beth when she needed her?

CHAPTER SIX

'WHAT DO YOU THINK YOU are doing?'

It wasn't so much a question as a cold and disapproving statement, Grace acknowledged with a wince as she cracked open one eyelid and found herself looking up at a grim-faced Cesar Navarro as he loomed over where she lay in the sunshine beneath a huge palm tree, the grass warm beneath her. 'Relaxing?'

'You could have done that in the apartment,' he grated harshly. 'In fact, I believe I said as much earlier when I suggested you take a siesta.'

'That's right, Cesar, you suggested I take a siesta.' Grace sat up slightly to lean back on her elbows as she looked up at him, not at all reassured by the grim accusation in his harshly hewn face, those black eyes glittering, his hands clenched beside his denim clad thighs. 'And I did try resting in the apartment once I had showered and changed and all the preparations were finished for this evening. I just found it impossible to fall asleep in the middle of the day, with the sun shining outside.' She wrinkled her nose. 'I'm English, Cesar, and as such I've never taken an afternoon siesta in my life.'

'So you decided to come out here to the park instead!' Again it was an accusation rather than a question.

Grace sighed. 'I believe I've already had this conversation once with Raphael.' She gave a pointed glance to where she could see the other man standing alert and watchful in the shadows of the trees twenty or so feet away. 'He didn't approve of my going out for a walk, either.' She wrinkled her nose at the conversation she'd had with the bodyguard before leaving the apartment.

'But you came, anyway.' His voice was dangerously soft.

'Obviously.' Grace had been unable to resist the lure of the park across from Cesar's apartment once she had looked out of the window of her bedroom, its lush greenness beckoning after the hours she had spent on the aeroplane to get here. 'And just as obviously Raphael chose to come running to you about it,' she added with another disgusted glance at the other man.

Cesar stiffened. 'He reported your movements to me, yes.'

Grace sighed. 'I had assumed, from what you said earlier, that I was allowed a couple of hours to myself before I need to cook dinner this evening?'

'Yes, of course.'

She nodded. 'And I chose to spend those hours sitting in the park.'

'You could have looked at the park from the windows of the apartment.'

'I didn't fly all this way to look at Buenos Aires through a window!' She gave an impatient shake of her head. 'You just don't get it, do you, Cesar? It's a beautiful sunny day, there's a park just across the road from your apartment— why wouldn't I want to come outside and breathe in the fresh air and explore a little?'

'Because it is not safe.'

'Oh, for goodness' sake!' Grace sat up fully to wrap her arms about her bent knees as she glared up at him. 'It's a public park, full of people walking their dogs, and couples and families enjoying themselves. Which is what I was also doing until a few minutes ago,' she added wearily.

His nostrils flared. 'Until I arrived.'

'Yes.' Not that Grace hadn't been expecting something like this; Raphael had made his disapproval of her plans more than obvious earlier, and she had seen him talking into his radio as he followed her across to the park, no doubt informing Cesar Navarro of exactly where she was going. 'You do know how ridiculous all of this is, don't you?'

Cesar's breath left him in a hiss, a nerve pulsing in his tightly clenched jaw as he stared down at her in frustration. 'You have no idea what you are talking about.'

'No?' She arched one sable brow.

'No.'

'Then explain it to me?'

His eyes glittered down at her. 'No.'

'This is just ridiculous.' She gave a helpless shake of her head. 'I doubt Fort Knox is as heavily guarded as you are! That's your choice, of course, but I draw the line at having my own movements curtailed in the same way yours are. Look around you, Cesar.' Her eyes glowed with pleasure as she did exactly that. 'It's beautiful here, peaceful and relaxing. Don't you ever take the time off from working to just sit back and smell the roses?'

His mouth twisted derisively. 'There are no roses where you are sitting.'

She shot him a reproving glance with those blue-green eyes. 'You pedant. You know exactly what I meant!'

Yes, he did, but the structure of Cesar's life did not allow for sitting back and smelling the roses; how could it, when he had an international business empire to run?

Something he had found impossible to continue doing

once informed by his Head of Security that Grace Blake had refused to remain in the apartment when advised to do so, and had instead gone outside for a walk in the park opposite! 'You will return to the apartment with me now.' He held out his hand with the intention of helping her to her sandalled feet.

A hand she ignored as she instead rested her chin on her bent knees and stared off into the distance. 'I think,' she said slowly, 'that once we get back to England, you should ask Kevin Maddox to find a replacement for me as quickly as possible.'

Cesar's brows rose as he allowed his hand to fall back to his side. 'You are terminating your employment with me?'

'Yes.'

'Because I am concerned for your safety?'

'No.' Tears swam in those blue-green eyes as she looked up at him, her sable hair falling silkily over her shoulders and down her back. 'I'm terminating my employment with you because I can't live like this.' Her voice was husky.

'You—'

'I feel like I'm being suffocated, Cesar!' she told him emotionally. 'Like that bird in a gilded cage—although in this case, it's obviously a pure gold one, with every luxury catered for. Except freedom.' She gave another shake of her head. 'How do you live like this, Cesar? Why do you live like this?'

Cesar stared down at her wordlessly for several long seconds, his frustration with her stubbornness warring with the need he felt to erase the bewilderment from Grace's expression and the tears from those beautiful sea-green eyes. 'As you said, it was a long flight here, you have not rested, and you are obviously overtired.'

'Oh, I'm way beyond tired,' she assured him heavily. 'I just want to get this month's employment over with and then go home. To my home. In London.' She turned her face away from him as she rested her cheek against her bent knees.

Cesar felt a painful jolt in his chest as he saw the slenderness of her shoulders shaking. 'Grace, are you crying?'

'No.' She sniffled.

'Yes.'

'Yes,' she conceded with a throaty sob.

Cesar dropped down onto his knees on the grass beside her before taking her in his arms and holding the stiffness of her body against his chest. 'There is no reason to cry, Grace,' he groaned as he rested his cheek against the top of her head, allowing him to breathe in the fragrance of silky dark hair.

'Of course there is,' she said with another sniffle.

'And why is that?' His fingers gently stroked the long length of that sable darkness.

Why? Grace wondered achingly. So many reasons, both logical and illogical, that she didn't know where to start. But first and foremost was that, illogically, she didn't really want to stop working for Cesar, that she actually enjoyed their verbal exchanges, enjoyed him. At least, she enjoyed those all too few brief moments when she succeeded in getting beneath the cool remoteness that he wore like a cloak over his emotions.

At the same time as she knew, logically, that she hated every moment of being constantly watched, by Raphael and his security team, as well as all those security cameras. So much so that she really was starting to feel suffocated by it all.

'Raphael is watching,' she reminded him gruffly.

'Not this time,' Cesar assured her dryly.

She raised her head to look across to where Raphael

had been standing, only to find that the other man was nowhere in sight. 'Where did he go?'

'I dismissed him when you began to cry.'

'I bet he was thrilled about that!'

'No doubt,' Cesar drawled.

'I—' She had glanced up at him—and instantly wished that she hadn't.

Cesar was much too close. Those sculpted lips were much too close. Mere inches away from her own as Cesar held her against him, the softness of his breath ruffling the tendrils of hair on her forehead as those jet-black eyes looked down into her own.

At that moment, as far as Grace was concerned, it felt as if there were only the two of them in the park, gazes locked, her breasts crushed against the hardness of Cesar's chest, the warmth of his hands on her back penetrating the light wool of her blue sweater, their thighs almost but not quite touching.

She drew in a ragged breath before moistening her lips with the tip of her tongue, not knowing what she was going to say, but feeling she had to say something to break the strained—expectant?—tension between them—

'Do not do that!' Cesar groaned huskily.

She stilled. 'Do what?'

'This!' His head bent and angled slightly so that the moistness of his tongue replaced her own as it swept slowly—arousingly!—across her lips. 'You have no idea how tempted I have been this past few days to taste you in just this way,' he murmured gruffly.

Grace looked up at him with wide eyes as she continued to breathe shallowly. 'You have?'

He gave a hard smile. 'Yes.'

She struggled to swallow. 'I didn't know.'

Of course she hadn't known; Cesar had become very

adept these last twenty years at hiding, controlling, his emotions, allowing nothing and no one to pierce that control. Except Grace Blake, with her pert outspokenness, and her unusual beauty, had been doing exactly that since the moment they first met.

To the extent that he had just dismissed his Head of Security and the two of them were now alone together in a very public park!

He allowed his arms to drop back to his sides before rising abruptly to his feet. 'It is time to go, Grace.' He looked down at her beneath hooded lids, not offering his hand this time but thrusting them into the pockets of his denims, not trusting himself in that moment to so much as touch her again when he could still taste the sweetness of her lips on his tongue.

She blinked before slowly rising to her feet beside him, her gaze no longer meeting his. 'Before Raphael has a heart attack.' She made an attempt at her usual dry humour.

'Yes.' Cesar gave a hard smile of acknowledgement. 'We will leave discussing the subject of if or when you leave my employment until after we have returned to England.' It was another statement rather than a question.

Not that Grace felt in any condition to answer him anyway; her heart was thundering so loudly in her chest she felt sure Cesar must be able to hear it, too, as the two of them walked side by side along the pathway leading back to his apartment.

Exactly what had happened just now? Had Cesar really been tempted these past few days to run his tongue—that sensuously arousing tongue!—across and between her lips? If he had, it was a temptation—and an admission—he obviously regretted, the handsomeness of his aristocratic face now set in its usual haughtily remote expression when Grace gave him a sideways glance.

Maybe it hadn't really happened? Maybe she had imagined—

No, she hadn't imagined anything, could still feel the soft rasp of Cesar's tongue against her lips. Could still taste his minty, spicy flavour on her mouth. Could still feel her response to that intimacy, her nipples pebble hard inside her lacy bra, between her thighs feeling uncomfortably hot and aroused.

It didn't help that once they had entered the apartment building and stepped into the lift together Grace instantly found herself remembering earlier today, when the circle of Cesar's arms had held her prisoner against the glass wall behind her and she had thought he was about to kiss her.

The cold remoteness of his expression as he stood grimly silent beside her assured Grace that there would be no repeat of that intimacy now. Cesar nodded curt dismissal of her once they were inside his apartment, before striding off down the hallway ahead of the waiting—and obviously grimly disapproving!—Raphael, the other man levelling a dark glower in Grace's direction before turning sharply on his heel and following their employer.

A glower that would no doubt have been even more disapproving if Raphael had witnessed his boss taking Grace in his arms before running the moistness of his tongue in a sensually sweeping caress against and between her lips…

'Grace, my guests have asked to meet you so that they might express their enjoyment of this evening's meal.'

She glanced across the kitchen at Cesar as he stood to one side to allow a smiling Maria to leave the room carrying the tray of coffee things through to the dining-room. Grace's breath hitched in her throat as she took in his appearance; he looked sinfully, powerfully handsome in his tailored black evening suit, snowy white shirt, and black bow tie, the darkness of his hair thick and glossy against the collar of that shirt.

It was the first time Grace had seen him since they had parted so abruptly earlier this afternoon. After Grace had told him she didn't feel she could carry on working for him. When Cesar, after holding her in his arms and running the sensual warmth of his tongue over and against her lips, had walked away from her without so much as a backward glance.

'Your chocolate mousse, as I had expected, was most especially appreciated,' he added dryly.

'Lucky you.' Grace gave a tight smile as she removed the apron from about her waist and placed it over the back of one of the kitchen chairs, once again wearing her uniform of a white blouse and pencil-slim knee-length skirt, the long length of her hair secured in a plait down her back this evening.

Cesar stilled, his eyes narrowing. 'Lucky me?'

Grace tossed that plait back over her shoulder as she straightened. 'The last time we spoke on the subject you appeared to think my chocolate mousse had sexual qualities.'

'Yes.'

She shrugged. 'Then let's hope it has set the mood for your female guest.'

'The mood for what?' Cesar thought he knew where this conversation was going, but he wanted to make sure he hadn't misunderstood her.

Grace gave him an exasperated glance. 'Seduction, of course!'

'Seduction?' he repeated slowly.

She nodded abruptly. 'It is your birthday, after all!'

Cesar arched one dark brow. 'And you believe it was

my intention to ply my female guest with your chocolate mousse and then seduce her at the end of the evening?'

She gave a dismissive snort. 'I thought that was the general idea, yes.'

Cesar didn't know whether to be amused or insulted. Insulted because Grace Blake believed he would ever need to use food—even her sinfully decadent chocolate mousse!—to seduce a woman into sharing his bed. Amusement because— Well, Grace Blake was about to learn the reason for his amusement!

'Come and meet my guests.' He stood back to allow her to precede him out of the kitchen, a hard smile curving his lips as he followed her down the length of the hallway to the dining-room, so distracted by the perfect curve of her bottom outlined against her black skirt that he almost walked into the back of her as she came to an abrupt halt in the doorway of the dining-room.

Grace was totally disconcerted by the two people seated at the table Maria had set earlier with silver flatware and crystal glasses.

The man was probably in his late fifties or early sixties, tall and dark-haired, a touch of distinguished grey at his temples, with jet-black eyes in a sculptured and handsome face; a physical likeness so similar to Cesar that the two men had to be related.

The woman seated beside him was probably in her early to mid fifties; tall and very slender, the black fitted dress she wore a perfect foil for her chic cap of pale blonde hair. There was no single feature that proclaimed her as also being related to Cesar, and her eyes were a warm blue in her smoothly beautiful face, and yet again Grace felt that jolt of recognition.

Cesar's hand was pressed against the small of Grace's back as he gently pushed her further into the room. 'Come and be introduced to my parents,' he drawled mockingly as Grace turned to look at him with accusing eyes.

Grace had spent most of the evening imagining Cesar in the dining-room charming the beautiful woman he intended taking to his bed later that night, and all the time his two dinner guests had been his mother and father?

The parents who had separated several years after the death of their toddler daughter, when it became too painful for them to remain together, had come together this evening to celebrate their son's birthday?

Carlos Navarro stood up politely as Grace reached the table and Cesar made the introductions. 'The meal was excellent, Miss Blake.' He gave her a courtly bow.

'It sure was.' Esther Navarro smiled as she stood up to come round the table and kiss Grace more warmly on both cheeks. 'If you ever get tired of working for my son, then be sure and let me know.' She gave the scowling Cesar a teasing glance before turning back to Grace. 'New York would just love you, Grace; have you ever been there?'

'Er—no,' she answered stiltedly, still feeling slightly wrong-footed by the identity of Cesar's dinner guests, even more so by Esther Navarro's obvious warmth of nature. A warmth and openness that was so much in contrast to her politely reserved husband and coldly remote son.

'You'd just love it, honey,' the older woman assured her.

'Stop trying to steal my employees, Mama,' Cesar drawled dryly. 'Grace lives with her younger sister in London, and has no interest in relocating to America.'

Grace was very aware that the warmth of his hand still rested against her lower back, almost but not quite touching the curve of her bottom.

As aware as she was that she had made a complete fool of herself a few minutes ago with her comments about chocolate mousse and seduction.

As aware as she was, from the amused glitter in Cesar's eyes now as he looked down at her, that he was completely aware of those feelings of embarrassment, and the reason for them!

Her back stiffened resolutely. 'Maybe Beth would like to go with me? I'm sure she would love the chance to work for a New York publisher.' She barely resisted gasping out loud as Cesar's response was to allow his hand to move slowly downwards until it lightly gripped one cheek of her bottom. 'Or not…' Grace added faintly, hoping—praying!—that neither Esther nor Carlos Navarro was aware of their son's overfamiliarity towards the woman who was his cook.

'Go get another cup from the kitchen, Cesar, and bring it through to the drawing-room?' Esther Navarro prompted lightly. 'Then Grace can join us all for coffee while I try to persuade her into coming back to New York with me. Or, at the very least, giving me the recipe for her chocolate mousse!' she added with a chuckle.

'Oh, I couldn't possibly—'

'Cesar?' his mother repeated with gentle firmness over Grace's protest.

'There really is no need for you to persuade me into anything,' Grace assured her quickly. 'I'll be quite happy to write out the recipe for the chocolate mousse and Ces— Mr Navarro—' she gave a wince at her slip '—can give it to you tomorrow.'

A slip Esther Navarro was only too aware of if the speculation in those warm blue eyes was any indication. 'Carlos?' she prompted her husband lightly.

'You will quickly learn, as we all have, that it is easier to give in to my wife than to fight her, Miss Blake,' Carlos Navarro said with obvious affection, before turning smilingly to his son. 'Another cup, Cesar.'

Cesar's fingers gave one last warning—just short of painful—squeeze of Grace's bottom, before he released her and stepped back. 'As my father said, it is far easier to simply acquiesce when my mother makes up her mind to do something,' he agreed with that same affection, but still managing to give Grace one last mocking glance before turning and leaving the dining-room in search of the requested fourth coffee cup.

She turned to give Esther Navarro an admiring glance. 'I'll happily give you the recipe for the chocolate mousse right now if you'll only tell me how you did that!'

The older woman gave a throaty chuckle. 'Like his father, Cesar's bark is much worse than his bite!' She linked her arm through Grace's. 'Now let's go and make ourselves cosy on the sofa in the drawing-room and visit for a while.'

Two hours, a pot of Cesar Navarro's special blend of coffee and a glass of brandy later, and Grace knew that 'visiting' with his mother consisted of pleasant conversation that was nevertheless designed to draw her guests into talking about themselves and their families, interspersed with laughter, as Esther related several amusing stories from Cesar's childhood.

Stories that had made Cesar squirm, and that contained no mention of the little girl the Navarro family had lost.

Nevertheless, Grace felt totally relaxed in Esther Navarro's company by the time the older couple departed, as if she had known the other woman for years.

'Leave that for now.'

Grace was in the process of tidying the coffee cups onto the tray when Cesar returned to the lamplit drawing-room after escorting his parents down to their car. She straightened to look across at him quizzically as he moved to pour two more glasses of brandy. 'They still love each other.'

'Yes,' he confirmed huskily as he handed her one of the glasses.

'Is there no chance they—?' She broke off, realising that she was broaching a very private subject to the Navarro family.

'That they might be reconciled?' Cesar finished wistfully, running a hand through the tousled length of his dark hair. 'After all this time, I think not. They meet once a year for my birthday.' He gave Grace an apologetic grimace for not revealing the identity of his guests to her earlier. 'Stay the night together at my father's home in the City, and then the following day my mother returns to New York.'

'But surely, if they love each other— I'm sorry, please just tell me to mind my own business if I'm being too personal?' She looked up at him anxiously.

He removed his jacket and bow tie, undoing the top button of his shirt as he shrugged to ease the tension out of his shoulders before indicating they should both sit down. 'How can I possibly do that when my own mother took great delight in relating to you the incident when I dived into the school pool and lost my swimming trunks?' He made himself comfortable in the chair across from Grace's.

She gave a soft chuckle. 'That was rather funny.'

'Not at the time,' he drawled. 'Perhaps if I had not attended a co-educational school!'

Cesar listened with pleasure as Grace gave another throaty chuckle. She had been tense and a little uncomfortable when she first joined them in the drawing-room for coffee, but his mother, one of the most warm and genuinely charming women Cesar had ever known, had soon put Grace at her ease.

It had been—despite his mother's insistence in telling amusing stories of his childhood—one of the most relaxed and pleasant birthday evenings he had ever spent, with none of the underlying memories of Gabriela hovering just beneath the surface of their every conversation. And he knew he had Grace's presence to thank for much of that.

Cesar looked at her over the rim of his brandy glass, pleased that she looked less tired and strained than she had earlier, despite having spent several hours cooking a magnificent meal for them all. 'Thank you for helping to make this such a memorable evening,' he murmured softly.

She gave him a startled glance. 'The fact that you all so obviously enjoyed your meal is thanks enough.'

Cesar shook his head. 'I was not referring to just the meal.'

Grace looked across at him uncertainly. It had been a strange and yet enjoyable evening, surprisingly so considering the tension between herself and Cesar earlier. 'Your parents are utterly charming,' she murmured non-committally.

He gave a tight smile. 'Surprisingly so, considering their son is not?'

Her cheeks felt warm. 'I don't recall ever saying that.'

'You did not need to.' Cesar continued to watch her intently over the rim of his brandy glass.

'Well, groping my backside when I was talking with your parents wasn't exactly charming, no.' She attempted to lighten the conversation.

He arched one dark brow. 'You know exactly why I did that.'

Grace snorted. 'Your mother wasn't really serious about my leaving your employment and moving to New York.'

'You obviously do not know my mother very well!' He gave a rueful shake of his head. 'The slightest encouragement on your part and you would have found yourself living in New York before the month was over!'

'Oh.'

'Yes.' He smiled slightly at her surprise. 'And would you have found my caressing your bottom more charming, if it had not happened in the presence of my parents?'

Grace's heart skipped a beat. 'No,' she answered firmly even as she placed her brandy glass down on the table beside her before standing up and moving to the low glass coffee table. 'I think I should just finish clearing away here and get to—' She broke off, her breath caught in her throat, as Cesar sat forward and reached out to grasp her wrist. 'Cesar?'

Those jet-black eyes were unreadable as he looked up to meet her gaze. 'Earlier this evening you asked me why it is I have the security that I do.'

She gave a shake of her head. 'I shouldn't have done that. I'm sorry.'

'Are you?'

'Yes.' She sighed. 'It was very rude of me.'

Cesar's thumb moved in a light caress against the pulse leaping in her wrist. 'It was a perfectly legitimate comment.' He gave a heavy sigh as he seemed to be searching for words. 'I—'

'Please, Cesar, you really don't owe me any explanations!'

Grace's nerves felt completely jittery, from that light caress on her hand and Cesar's light grasp of her fingers.

'Yes, I believe that I do.' His eyes glittered pure jet as he looked up at her. 'Not many people are aware of this but—' He broke off to draw in a deep ragged breath, lines of grief etched beside his eyes and mouth. 'My sister, Gabriela—'

'Please don't, Cesar!' Grace's fingers tightened about his as she silenced him. 'I shouldn't have spoken to you in the way that I did earlier, and you certainly don't owe me any explanations for the way you choose to live your life.

Or to bring back painful memories by talking of your sister's death.' She gave a self-disgusted shake of her head.

His breath left him in a hiss. 'Gabriela did not die, Grace. Or, at least, it has always been my hope, despite some of the alternatives, that she did not,' he added in a pained voice.

'But you said—' Grace felt utterly bewildered by this conversation. She had thought—believed that Cesar had placed a wall about his emotions, that his parents' marriage had eventually been destroyed, by the death of two-year-old Gabriela twenty-one years ago. 'I don't understand, Cesar?'

Those lines deepened beside his eyes and mouth. 'My sister, Gabriela, was taken from us,' he revealed gruffly.

'Taken?' Grace breathed softly.

Cesar nodded. 'Whilst in a park very much like the one in which you sat this afternoon,' he added in husky apology.

Grace stared down at him in utter shock. She had assumed, when Cesar had talked of the loss of his sister, that Gabriela Navarro had died. A terrible tragedy, and one that had eventually ripped Gabriela's family apart.

But, if she understood Cesar correctly now—and Grace felt sure that she did—that wasn't what had happened at all.

Gabriela Navarro hadn't died.

She had been taken.

Abducted…

CHAPTER SEVEN

'MY GOD, CESAR!' Grace choked emotionally as she dropped down onto the carpet beside his chair to grasp his hand tightly in both of hers as she looked up at him. 'I can't believe—Gabriela was kidnapped…?'

Cesar's expression softened slightly as he saw the tears of empathy shimmering in Grace's blue-green eyes. 'Taken,' he insisted gruffly.

'How? Where?'

'We had gone to the park with our niñera— Yes,' Cesar gave an acknowledging grimace as Grace gasped at he once again mentioned the park. 'It was April, a time when the pollen would not bother Gabriela—'

'She's the one who's allergic to flowers?' she breathed softly.

He gave another acknowledging nod. 'I have not been able to bear having flowers inside the house since she disappeared.'

And Grace had thought he was just being unreasonable that first day at his estate when he had asked for the flowers to be removed from the entrance hall, and again earlier today when she had accused him of once again being paranoid because she had chosen to go into the park opposite this apartment.

He sighed. 'We played with Gabriela in the park for an

hour or so chasing a ball, until she became tired and fell asleep in her pushchair, finally allowing me to fly the kite I had received as an Easter gift.' Cesar's gaze was unfocused as he obviously relived a day he would never forget. 'The wind was too strong, the string broke, and my kite drifted off to become entangled in some bushes a short distance away. Our niñera was only distracted from Gabriela for one minute, perhaps two, when she came to help untangle the kite, but when she turned to where she had been sitting Gabriela's pushchair was empty,' he concluded bleakly. 'We both searched for her, becoming more frantic by the moment, believing she must have woken up and wandered off somewhere but—she was gone. Disappeared as if from the face of the earth.'

Leaving Cesar to spend the rest of his life knowing it had been his enjoyment of flying his kite that had allowed the opportunity for Gabriela to be taken?

'My parents were beside themselves with grief as we waited for the ransom to be demanded,' he continued, his voice raw with emotion. 'We all waited, hours, days, weeks. But there was nothing. Just an empty space where our Gabriela should have been,' he recalled bleakly.

Grace's throat moved as she swallowed before speaking, the tears falling unchecked down her cheeks now. 'But—it was never reported in the newspapers…' She had no doubts it would have been in the article she had read online about Cesar if that had been the case.

He gave a shake of his head. 'My father was, and still is, a very powerful man in Argentina, and he believed it would be safer for Gabriela if her disappearance was not allowed to become a public media circus.'

'But surely the police—' She broke off as Cesar gave another shake of his head.

He sighed. 'Again, rightly or wrongly, my father refused to involve them at first, believed that by doing so he would be putting Gabriela's life at risk. And so we waited, each sleepless night and day more torturous than the last, for the phone call or letter which would tell us that Gabriela was still alive, and would be returned safely to us if the money was paid. It never came,' he breathed harshly. 'There was nothing but silence, the same silence which has existed for the past twenty-one years,' he revealed with that same raw emotion.

Grace moistened her lips. 'What do you think happened to her?'

His eyes glittered fiercely. 'I have tried not to think too deeply about that, for fear I might go mad.'

Grace didn't know what to say. What could she possibly say about the nightmare the Navarro family had lived with for the past twenty-one years? Their daughter taken from them, not dead, but as lost to them as if she were. As Grace knew only too well after the death of both her adoptive parents, painful as it was, there was at least closure with death; the Navarro family hadn't had that, would never have that, because they had no idea whether Gabriela had died or was living her life somewhere else right now, in total ignorance of their very existence, or heartbreak.

'By the time my father agreed to call in the police the trail was cold,' Cesar continued flatly, his gaze still distant with memories. 'Oh, they followed up every report they received of a golden-haired two-year-old-girl child, and we waited and prayed, but it was never Gabriela. And my mother died a little more inside with each raising of those hopes before they were so quickly followed by devastating disappointment when it was not her daughter.'

'And the rift between her and your father grew wider,' Grace guessed huskily.

Cesar focused on her with effort. 'Yes. And I—' He

broke off to draw in a deep and shuddering breath. 'You can have no idea of the torment of all these years, of looking at every blonde-haired dark-eyed girl and woman I met, and wondering if this could be Gabriela, grown up and beautiful, but with no knowledge or memory of her true family. How could she have, when she had been only two when she was taken from us?'

And this was the man Grace had believed to be not only paranoid, but cold and unemotional. Cesar wasn't any of those things, he had just learnt to control and contain his emotions, for fear that if he once allowed them full rein he would be totally overwhelmed by them.

'I can understand a little.' Grace nodded. 'I know it isn't quite the same.' She grimaced. 'But—I was eight when my parents adopted five-year-old Beth, and decided to tell me that I was adopted, too.' She gave a shake of her head. 'Oh, they did it the usual way, explained how special I was, that they had chosen me as their daughter. But after that I—I began to look at the people I met, couples I would see in the street, and in restaurants and hotels, and wonder if they might be my birth parents,' she admitted gruffly.

Cesar moved his hand up to smooth back the tendrils of hair at her temples. 'It would seem that we are more alike than we might ever have realised,' he murmured ruefully.

Grace's choked laugh was completely spontaneous. 'Oh, yes, we're very alike! You're Cesar Navarro, the successful businessman and billionaire,' she explained at his questioning look. 'And I'm Grace Blake, the cordon bleu chef who currently can't even get a job in a London hotel or restaurant!'

'Those things are what we are on the outside, Grace.' The darkness of his gaze held hers captive. 'Inside, we are both of us searching for an elusive something we believe might help to complete us.'

The air around them had become so tense in the last few minutes, so heavy with emotion, that Grace found she was still crying. And she couldn't she look away from the dark intensity of Cesar's gaze.

'Please do not cry, Grace. I cannot bear to see you cry!' His thumb moved gently across her tear-wet cheeks before both his hands moved up to cradle each side of her face as he slowly lowered his head and claimed the softness of her lips with his own.

A kiss so poignantly beautiful that Grace found it impossible not to respond as his lips gently sipped and tasted her own.

A kiss that didn't stay poignant or gentle as Cesar gave a groan deep in this throat, his hands leaving the sides of her face as he drew her up into his arms. Grace was now sitting on his muscled thighs as his fingers became entangled in the heavy darkness of her hair and he angled her face to allow him to deepen the kiss with the moist sweep of his tongue across her parted lips.

Grace groaned low in her throat as she turned fully in his arms, her breasts pressed against the heat of Cesar's chest she could feel through the thin silk of his shirt, as she finally threaded her fingers into the silky darkness of that dark and tousled hair and returned the heat of those kisses.

Deep, searching kisses that quickly raged out of control as Cesar turned slightly in the chair and lay Grace back against his arm about her shoulders, the better to allow him to devour the softness of her lips as he drew in her brandy and peaches taste of her tongue duelling with his. Her perfume was an insidious combination of flowers and hot, aroused woman as Cesar's free hand roamed restlessly across the curviness of her hips and slenderness of her waist before lightly cupping beneath the swell of her breast.

A full and aroused breast, that allowed him to feel the

press of swollen nipple through her blouse and lacy bra.
A lacy bra that had driven Cesar to distraction earlier this
evening as they talked with his parents and he caught
tantalising glimpses of that lace against and beneath her
blouse.

She gasped softly as Cesar ran the soft pad of his thumb
across that swollen berry, only to gasp and press up and
into him as he repeated that caress, her bottom shifting
restlessly against his arousal as he repeated that caress
again and again whilst continuing to devour the sweet in-
toxication of her lips and mouth.

Grace groaned low in her throat as Cesar squeezed and
caressed the aching tip of her breast, wanting—oh, hell,
wanting— 'Cesar!' she pleaded breathlessly as his lips left
hers and moved along the column of her throat and up to
latch onto the sensitive lobe of her ear, teeth gently biting,
and sending quivers of pleasure to the tips of her breasts
and the swollen heat between her thighs. 'Cesar, please!'
she groaned achingly. 'Yes!' That groan turning to a hiss-
ing release of satisfaction as he pulled her blouse free from
the waistband of her skirt and she felt the warmth of his
hand against her own heated flesh, her waist, her ribs, before he finally cupped her lace-covered breast, squeezing
gently before pushing the lacy cup downward and under
her breast as he bared that turgid nipple to his caresses.

Grace's insides turned to liquid fire as Cesar's lips once
again travelled the length of her throat as he rolled that
bared and swollen nipple between thumb and finger, lightly
and then harder, caressing, squeezing, pulling almost to
the point of pain, before repeating that first light caress.

Grace was held captive by the dark heat in Cesar's eyes
as he deftly unfastened the buttons of her blouse before
pushing it to one side, his gaze lowering as he revealed the
full swell of her breast tipped with that deep rose nipple.

'Beautiful…' he groaned, his hand capturing and holding that creaminess as his head slowly lowered.

Grace lay back and watched in fascination as the warmth of Cesar's lips moved across that swell, tasting, licking, but never quite touching the ache of her throbbing nipple. 'Please, Cesar!' She arched her back and lifted up to him when she couldn't bear the teasing torment any longer, and was instantly rewarded as he parted his lips over that pert nipple before suckling her into the moist heat of his mouth, and sending waves of that heat deep between her throbbing thighs.

Cesar suckled hungrily on Grace's sweetness, pulling her ever deeper into the heat of his mouth, tongue rasping that aroused nipple, teeth gently biting to the throb of his aroused and pulsing shaft against the pertness of the bottom he had touched and so fleetingly squeezed earlier tonight. He realised that Grace's hands hadn't been idle as he felt the caress of her fingers against his own bared chest. Fleeting, light caresses as she traced the hard contours of his muscled shoulders and chest.

He became lost in the pleasure of those caresses as her fingers lightly grazed his sensitive flesh before moving lower, those rousing fingertips dancing over the muscled contours of his stomach, following that line of dark hair, which formed a perfect V down beneath the waistband of his trousers, before she cupped the length of his aroused shaft in the palm of her hand.

Cesar raised his head reluctantly as Grace would have unfastened his trousers, his ragged breathing sounding harshly in the otherwise silence of the room. 'We must stop now, Grace.' He placed a kiss on each ruby-red nipple before gently straightening her bra and pulling the two sides of her blouse together to cover her nakedness.

'What?' Grace looked up at him with dark, unfocused

eyes, her lips full and swollen from their kisses, her cheeks flushed with arousal.

'The security camera—' He broke off as she gasped before sitting up abruptly.

Grace's eyes were wide with shock as she scrambled off Cesar's thighs and stood up, holding her unbuttoned blouse tightly across the swell of her breasts, her face pale as she looked across the room at the security camera.

The security camera!

All the time she had been in Cesar's arms that damned security camera had been recording everything they did. When Cesar had unbuttoned her blouse, bared her breasts, kissed her breasts, and suckled her nipples!

And someone—Raphael?—would have been watching all of those things as they happened.

She turned back to Cesar as he sat forward tensely in the armchair, the darkness of his hair even more sexily tousled than usual from where her fingers had threaded through it earlier, his eyes dark and unfathomable, his cheeks flushed, his unbuttoned shirt revealing the bronzed skin of his bared chest with its covering of silky dark hair.

Her angry gaze flashed back to his face. 'How could you do that to me?' she choked out.

He frowned darkly as he stood up quickly. 'Grace.'

'How could you?' Her breasts—breasts that still ached from Cesar's ministrations—quickly rose and fell in her agitation as she quickly refastened her blouse.

His mouth tightened. 'I simply forgot the camera was there.'

'You forgot?' she repeated incredulously. 'You live with those damned cameras twenty-four hours a day, but tonight you just forgot about them?'

'Yes, Grace, I forgot.' A nerve pulsed in the tightness of his jaw as he ran an agitated hand through the tousled darkness of his hair. 'The moment I kissed you everything else went out of my head.'

'Really?' Grace scorned, knowing she was being unreasonable, unfair even, but too embarrassed, by the thought of Raphael or one of the other security guards watching her and Cesar together, to think of anything else at that moment.

'Yes, really,' Cesar bit out harshly, those dark eyes glittering dangerously. 'I accept it was a serious omission on my part, Grace…' his voice softened '…but you are behaving irrationally—'

'No, Cesar, I'm behaving exactly in the way any woman would at the thoughts of someone—some—some voyeur!—watching the two of us—the two of us— I want that security disc destroyed, Cesar!' She was shaking with humiliation as she glowered across at him. 'Snapped in half, quarters—tiny little pieces!—and then incinerated. Do you hear me?'

He winced as her voice rose with each successive word. 'I believe the whole of Buenos Aires can hear you at this moment.'

'The whole of Buenos Aires is welcome to hear me at this moment!' Grace was breathing hard in her agitation. In her feelings of humiliation! She hadn't even been out on a date for over a year, and she had never, ever allowed a man to touch and kiss her as intimately as Cesar just had. 'Raphael, or one of his cohorts, will have seen all of that,' she groaned. 'How am I ever going to face him or them ever again? How?'

'Raphael is the soul of discretion—'

'And I suppose you know that because this sort of situation occurs on a regular basis? Maybe you even have your own private collection of—'

'I advise you to stop right there, Grace,' Cesar warned softly.

'And if I don't? What are you going to do to me, Cesar?' She glared at him. 'Fire me? Well, let me save you the bother—'

'Do not do or say anything in haste, Grace,' he warned chillingly.

'It isn't in haste, Cesar.' The tears in her eyes made it difficult for her to see him as any more than a hazy outline. 'I hate the way you live, the security guards, the cameras; I hate it all.'

'I—'

'Oh, I understand the reason for them, Cesar.' One hot, scalding tear escaped down the coolness of her cheeks. 'I understand completely now that I know why it is you choose to live like this. I just—I like being with people, Cesar. All types of people, the bad as well as the good, and I can't breathe in this ivory tower you've created to keep others out.' She drew in a shaky breath. 'I'm not going to just leave you without a cook or a housekeeper—that would be totally wrong. But I am giving you notice now, Cesar, that I won't be staying on when my one month's trial is over. That should give Kevin Maddox plenty of time to replace me.'

Cesar had no idea what to say, what to do—and no doubt Grace would tell him he had already done enough.

He hadn't meant to kiss Grace, certainly hadn't intended to make love to her in the way that he had, but her tears, the taste of her lips, the warmth of her response, had all served to shatter his usual self-control, to the point that he had briefly forgotten everything else.

With the result that Grace was now angry with him and embarrassed at the thought of having to face Raphael again.

He drew in a deep breath. 'I will speak to Raphael—'

'All the talking in the world isn't going to make him forget what he saw,' Grace said wearily, pushing back the loose tendrils of hair from her cheeks.

That same silky sable hair that Cesar had so enjoyed touching such a short time ago. And which his fingers still longed to touch. Instead he put those fingers to work re-fastening several buttons on his shirt. 'Perhaps we should discuss this again in the morning, when emotions are not running so high?'

She shot him a pitying glance. 'Whose emotions would those be, Cesar?'

His mouth thinned. 'Insulting me will do nothing to change the awkwardness of this situation, Grace.'

'No,' she conceded heavily. 'I'll finish clearing away now.' Her gaze avoided meeting his as she moved to pick up the tray of coffee things.

'Maria can do that in the morning.'

Grace gave a rueful smile. 'I made the mess—I clear it up.'

'You are exhausted.'

'And you really think I'm going to be able to sleep after this?' she demanded.

No more than Cesar was. Although the reasons for those feelings of sleeplessness were different: Grace was upset and embarrassed; Cesar was still aroused. Too much so to be able to go to his lonely bed and sleep.

'Goodnight, Cesar.'

He winced at the weary flatness of her tone. 'Goodnight, Grace.'

She had paused in the doorway. 'I—I would like to go out tomorrow and see some more of Buenos Aires before we leave.' She met his gaze challengingly. 'Beth didn't approve of my coming here but—'

'Why not?'

Grace gave a rueful smile. 'I don't think she liked the idea of my going away with a man—even one that's an employer—I've only just met.'

'A disapproval which just now would seem to justify?'

'Yes,' Grace confirmed huskily. 'Nevertheless, she would never forgive me if I didn't take her something back, and at least see some of the city while I'm here,' she added ruefully.

A city Cesar had no doubt Grace had no intention of ever returning to. 'I will see what can be arranged.' He nodded abruptly. 'Do not pressure me for an answer on this tonight, Grace,' he warned harshly as he saw the way her mouth had set in a stubborn line.

Grace looked at him searchingly, knowing by the dangerous glitter of those dark eyes, and the tensing of his already clenched jaw, that she really had pushed Cesar enough for one night, that his temper, usually so cold and controlled, was near to the surface as her own, and in danger of erupting with the destruction of a volcano's hot lava.

Not that she had any intention of allowing Cesar's disapproval of her plans to make the slightest difference to her own decision to venture out into the city tomorrow. She was going, and that was an end to the subject as far as she was concerned; she very much doubted she would ever have another chance to see Buenos Aires!

Grace nodded abruptly. 'I'll make sure everything is tidy in the kitchen before I go to bed.'

'I wish you sweet dreams, Grace.'

She turned back sharply. 'What did you say?'

He gave a shrug. 'When I was a child my mother always said that to me when I was going to bed. Did your mother not say the same thing to you?'

Her brows rose. 'Not that I recall, no. Nor is it particularly appropriate between the two of us right now,' she added ruefully.

'No.' Cesar grimaced as he thrust his hands into his trouser pockets. 'I will just wish you goodnight, then.'

'You already did that.'

'Then I must have meant it if I have just repeated it!' He bit out his frustration with the awkwardness that now existed between the two of them.

Grace continued to look at him for several seconds before giving an abrupt nod of her head. 'Goodnight, Cesar.' She walked out of the room and down the hallway to the kitchen.

A room that suddenly seemed empty, almost lonely, now that first his parents, and now Grace, had all gone. And Cesar was never lonely. Always alone, but never lonely...

He moved to the decanter of brandy and refilled his glass before striding restlessly across the room to stand in front of the window, his expression bleak as he found himself thinking of Grace rather than looking at the city of Buenos Aires spread out before him. A city Grace had decided she wished—fully intended, if he had heard her tone correctly!—to explore the following day. Something he could not allow. Unless—

'Cesar?'

He turned slowly, raising one dark questioning brow at Raphael as the other man stood in the shadows of the open doorway.

'Where is Señorita Blake...?'

'Grace has gone to bed, Raphael—as I am sure you are only too well aware,' Cesar answered him. 'Join me?' He held up his glass of brandy in invitation to the other man.

'*Gracias.*' Raphael stepped into the room and poured

himself a glass of the brandy before strolling over to stand beside Cesar in front of the window.

The two men were, as Grace had known intuitively, much more than employer and employee, but not in the way she had suspected; it was a bond of friendship only, one that had been forged during their years together at school, and Cesar had been more than happy to offer the other man the post of Head of Security ten years ago when Raphael, having recently left the army, told him how he could not live at his family's vineyards at Cuyo. The arrangement had worked very well for both men.

Raphael sipped his brandy. 'Miss Blake has a temper.'

Cesar found himself grinning appreciatively. 'Oh, yes.'

The other man nodded. 'I like that about her.'

'So, unfortunately, do I.' Cesar sighed heavily.

Raphael quirked a dark brow over piercing blue eyes. 'Unfortunately?'

Cesar gave a shrug of his shoulders. 'She not only has a temper but she is headstrong. She wishes to go and explore Buenos Aires tomorrow,' he explained impatiently.

'Then let her.'

'Alone,' Cesar added pointedly.

'Ah.' Raphael nodded in understanding. 'I am sure we will be able to accommodate her request.'

'And I am just as sure that Grace will do everything in her power to evade any attempt on your part to follow or have her followed,' he said knowingly.

Raphael pursed his lips in thought. 'Then we must find a way she will find acceptable.'

'I already have.'

The other man looked at him searchingly for several long seconds before his brow cleared and he gave a firm shake of his head. 'No, Cesar, I cannot allow—'

'It will be all right, old friend.' Cesar smiled at the other man reassuringly. 'Grace is right.' He frowned. 'I have built myself an ivory tower in which to live. One that is secure certainly, but which also prevents me from being part of the world around me.' He turned to look out of the window at the lights of Buenos Aires. 'Perhaps it is time for that to change.'

'I cannot express too strongly how much I disapprove —' Raphael broke off his protest to look enquiringly at Cesar as he chuckled softly.

'Do you really think that anyone would dare to approach Grace, let alone challenge her, in her present mood?' he drawled derisively.

The other man grimaced. 'It would take a braver man than I, certainly.'

'She has a younger sister.' Cesar arched a mocking brow.

'*Dios* protect me from beautiful headstrong women!' Raphael threw the rest of his brandy to the back of his throat before moving to place the empty glass on the coffee table. 'We will talk of this further tomorrow, Cesar?'

'We will.' He shrugged. 'And, Raphael—' he stopped the other man as he reached the doorway '—destroy the security disc from an hour ago,' he added grimly.

'*Sí.*' Raphael nodded before striding away.

Cesar turned back to look out of the window at Buenos Aires once more. His city.

A city he fully intended to explore at Grace's side the following day.

Whether she wished it or not.

And Cesar had no doubts that, after their intimacy tonight, she would not!

CHAPTER EIGHT

'WHY ARE YOU eating your breakfast in here?' Cesar stood in the doorway of the kitchen looking across at Grace through narrowed lids as she sat at the breakfast bar obviously enjoying eating her croissants and drinking coffee, the turquoise blouse she wore this morning a perfect match for the colour of her eyes.

He had expected, waited, for Grace to join him in the dining-room for breakfast, to give him the opportunity to tell her of the arrangements he had made for today. Instead of which Maria had informed him a few minutes ago, when she brought his own pot of coffee through to the dining-room, that Grace was at this moment eating her breakfast in the kitchen.

Grace had almost choked on the last of her croissant at the sound of Cesar's voice, taking a quick sip of her coffee now to help the pastry down her throat as she looked across the kitchen at him.

And instantly feeling as if she might choke again, this time from lack of oxygen. Cesar's appearance, in a short-sleeved black tee shirt that moulded to the muscled contours of his shoulders and chest, faded denims that fitted low down on the leanness of his hips, and scuffed black boots, totally took her breath away. Add tousled overlong dark hair, brooding black eyes, and those perfect chiselled features to the mix, and Cesar Navarro was enough to rob any female, nineteen to ninety, of her next breath!

Add to that the memory of those chiselled lips kissing and suckling her breasts the night before, and Grace found it difficult to breathe at all.

Sure that she wouldn't be able to sleep after leaving Cesar the night before, Grace had at first tossed and turned beneath the covers in her comfortable bed, only to eventually fall into a fitful and dream-filled sleep.

Such weird and disjointed dreams. Of running and running, with her hair streaming behind her, the softness of her nightgown billowing and then moulding to her as she searched and searched for something that couldn't be found, followed by a vision of a much younger Cesar playing in the park with a little blonde-haired angel, and a familiar voice whispering 'sweet dreams' as Grace ran past a vase of yellow roses swaying in a gentle breeze, a red-and-blue kite blowing above in that same breeze, and all of it watched by a pair of piercing and disembodied black eyes.

Then with the suddenness of dreams it had all changed and Grace had become aware of the sensual caress of hands and lips against the bareness of her skin, arousing her, sending her higher and higher towards—

She had woken so suddenly at that point that she had sat bolt upright in the bed, eyes wide, her breathing ragged, her body one hot and yearning ache, her breasts feeling full and her nipples engorged, and between her thighs swollen and damp.

It didn't need too much intelligence to understand what the latter part of her dream had been about—or to know that the reason for it was standing in the kitchen doorway at this very moment! And no doubt most of the earlier dream had some foundation in reality, the whole succeeding in keeping Grace awake for several more hours as she tried, and failed, to make sense of it. Consequently, she was feeling decidedly cranky this morning from too little sleep.

She was certainly in no mood to deal with Cesar's arrogance. 'Where else would I eat my breakfast?' She studiously rubbed the last of the pastry flakes from her fingers before standing to pick up her empty plate and mug and carry them across the kitchen to bend over to load them into the dishwasher, the loosened darkness of her hair falling forward and hiding her expression.

'In the dining-room with me.'

Grace straightened slowly, her eyes wide as she once again looked across the kitchen at Cesar. 'Why on earth would I do that?'

He scowled his impatience. 'Why would you not?'

'Well, let me see,' she replied crisply as she slipped her hands into the back pockets of her close-fitting jeans; there was absolutely no reason why she should allow Cesar to see that this meeting, the first after he had touched and kissed her so intimately the night before, was enough to make her hands visibly tremble! 'Firstly, I'm as much an employee here as Maria is, and so I wouldn't presume to eat breakfast with my employer—'

'You are in Argentina as my guest—'

'I'm in Argentina because I was cooking your birthday dinner last night.'

'And now it is the weekend, and so you are my guest.'

'I'm not cooking dinner this evening, too?'

He gave a shake of his head. 'Maria will cook dinner for us both this evening.'

Dinner for them both? Grace wasn't at all sure she felt comfortable with that.

'Secondly,' she continued firmly, 'I didn't want to eat breakfast with you.'

He drew in a sharp breath at her bluntness. 'You are still angry because of what happened last night?'

She gave a scornful snort. 'Now what on earth makes you think that?'

Cesar didn't think it—he knew it! It was there in the glitter of those blue-green eyes, and the firm set of her full and pouting lips—the same lips he had taken such pleasure in kissing the night before.

Unfortunately the pallor of Grace's cheeks, and the dark shadows beneath her eyes, also told him that she had not slept any better the night before than he had himself. 'Raphael has disposed of the relevant security footage.'

'I hope by that you mean he's incinerated it?' she came back challengingly.

'I do, yes,' Cesar confirmed tersely.

'Pity his memory of it can't be wiped out, too,' Grace said tartly.

Cesar drew in a controlling breath. 'Believe it or not, Raphael likes and respects you, and as such I have every confidence that he would never discuss or mention the events of last night, with anyone else.'

'And you're happy with that, are you?' Grace demanded.

'No, I am not happy—' Cesar broke off his angry reply to take in another slow and controlling breath. 'I have asked that all the cameras inside the apartment be switched off until after we have departed tomorrow.'

Her eyes widened. 'Why on earth would you—?' She gave a hard laugh. 'I seriously hope you didn't do that with any expectation of a repeat of last night, Cesar! Because if you did—'

'I may understand the reason for your displeasure, Grace, but that does not mean I am willing to allow you to continue insulting me indefinitely!' His patience had come to an abrupt end. 'I instructed the cameras be switched off because you stated you are uncomfortable with them, nothing more and nothing less.'

She raised dark brows. 'And Raphael just accepted that?'

He gave a hard smile. 'It would not be gentlemanly of me to repeat to you Raphael's response to my request.'

Grace didn't want to like this man—in fact, it would be so much better for her if she could dislike Cesar intensely!—but it was impossible not to feel a certain amount of gratitude for this unexpected act of sensitivity in regard to her stated dislike of those security cameras. And no doubt Raphael was even now rethinking that 'liking and respect' Cesar claimed the other man felt towards her.

She swallowed. 'I— That was…very thoughtful of you.'

He gave a hard smile. 'As much so as it was painful for you to acknowledge it.'

'You have no idea.'

'Oh, but I have,' Cesar assured her dryly as a wry smile curved his lips. 'Are you ready to leave now or do you need time to collect a jacket from your bedroom?' Much as he knew Grace would not appreciate the fact, Cesar was finding the outline of her bottom in those tight-fitting jeans a complete distraction from his decision to keep things light and friendly between them today. A jacket might help to hide that tempting curve from his vision!

'Ready?' she repeated warily.

Cesar gave an acknowledging inclination of his head. 'I am offering my services as your guide around the beautiful city of my birth.'

Grace was too stunned to hide that surprise. 'Why on earth would you do that?'

Cesar's mouth thinned. 'Because I wish to.'

Of course; Grace knew him well enough by now to know that Cesar never did anything he didn't want to do.

Nevertheless… 'It's very nice of you, to offer, but I would really prefer to go out on my own.'

His jaw tightened. 'Why?'

She sighed deeply. 'Probably because I don't want to be surrounded by a phalanx of security guards all day.'

'There will be no security guards today, Grace.'

'No security? You've dismissed them, too?' She all but gaped at him now.

'For today, yes,' Cesar confirmed with an abrupt inclination of his head. 'I will also be leaving my mobile phone here.'

'But why?' she gasped. 'You never go anywhere without security guards and your mobile phone!'

He gave a rueful smile. 'I believe you were the one who said that I miss much of the enjoyment of life that way?'

'Yes…'

'And also suggested that I needed to take time out to "smell the roses"?'

'Well. Yes, I said that, too. But—there's a vast difference between delicately smelling the roses and throwing yourself naked into the whole rose garden!' She looked at him exasperatedly.

He arched dark brows. 'I believe the latter would prove extremely painful, yes.'

'But I—' Grace gave a bewildered shake of her head, ignoring his derision. 'I don't know what to say.'

'As I have said before, an unusual occurrence, certainly, but I am sure it will very quickly pass,' he teased.

'This isn't funny, Cesar.' She frowned heavily.

'I agree, it is not.' He sobered. 'Perhaps it is that you do not wish to see Buenos Aires with me?'

'I would love to see Buenos Aires with someone who loves the city as much as you obviously do. I just— What if someone recognises you and decides to—to—? Well, I don't know what they might decide to do.' She waved an impatient hand.

'Raphael agreed with me on one thing, at least—that the fierceness of your expression would be enough to deter anyone from approaching either one of us today,' he explained at Grace's questioning look.

'Oh, very funny!' She gave him an exasperated glare.

Cesar gave a grin. 'We thought so, yes.'

'Raphael must really hate me at this moment!'

Cesar shrugged. 'He will get over it.'

Grace could only admire his confidence. 'Don't you need to spend time with your mother today?'

He gave a shake of his head. 'We said our goodbyes last night. She will be returning to New York on a flight later this afternoon.'

Grace's eyes widened. 'She really does only stay here long enough to celebrate your birthday?'

'Yes,' Cesar confirmed abruptly.

'That's—' Grace gave a pained frown. 'That's incredibly sad.'

'Yes. And today is not a day for sadness,' Cesar replied smoothly. 'So, do you need to collect a jacket or are you ready to leave now?'

After the embarrassment of last night Grace hadn't even known how she was going to face Cesar again today, and now, incredibly, she could feel a bubble of excitement rising inside her just at the thought of spending the day with him. Of strolling around Buenos Aires at Cesar's side. Just the two of them. Sans any security guards.

Still she hesitated. 'Are you absolutely sure about this?'

'Absolutely,' he echoed dryly.

Then obviously there was nothing else for Grace to do but go to her bedroom, tidy her appearance, and collect her jacket!

* * *

'You are very quiet.' Cesar looked down at Grace several hours later as the two of them strolled together through the streets of Buenos Aires.

She looked up at him with shining aquamarine eyes. 'It's all just so… I'm just bedazzled by the…the shops you took into were… I loved the museum… And that wonderful bookshop…and—'

'Perhaps I was a little hasty earlier when I assumed that your speechlessness would not last,' Cesar joked.

She rolled her eyes at him expressively. 'I had no idea Buenos Aires was so beautiful. That it was such a contrast of eclectic architecture and magnificent statuary, along with the most amazing shops and markets.'

Cesar gave a shrug of his shoulders beneath the black leather jacket he now wore over his tee shirt. 'We endeavour to keep the unique beauty of Argentina to ourselves as much as possible.'

Grace gave an appreciative chuckle. 'Pity, then, that when I get back to England I'm going to tell Beth and all of my friends that Buenos Aires, at least, is a place they just have to visit!'

Cesar raised a dark brow. 'You have many friends in England?'

'Quite a few,' she answered after several seconds' thought. 'From school, you know, and from working in the kitchen in hotels in France and England.'

He nodded slowly. 'Raphael and I were at school together.'

Her eyes widened. 'You were?'

Cesar smiled at her obvious surprise. 'Yes.'

'But you went to a private school, didn't you?'

'Yes.'

'Then why does Raphael now work as your—?'

'I do not discuss the personal lives of my friends, Grace,' he cut in dismissively.

'No. Of course not.' Grace nodded, realising from the flatness of Cesar's tone that it was time to change the subject. 'Are we nearly at the market you told me about, where you think I might be able to buy something to take home for Beth?'

'Feria de San Pedro Telmo.' Cesar nodded. 'It is not far from here.'

'Oh, my goodness!' Grace gasped as they literally turned a corner and she found herself looking at the most colourful buildings she had ever seen in her life: zinc shacks and houses painted in the bright colours of every shade of blue, green, red, yellow, and all the colours in between.

'San Telmo,' Cesar supplied with satisfaction.

Grace had never seen anywhere quite like this before, every bench lining the street and every conceivable piece of space on every building painted in an array of colours that should have looked garish and yet didn't. Instead those bright colours were a pleasure to the senses, a fact appreciated by the dozens of people sitting in the many crowded outside cafés and restaurants.

'Would you like to sit and have a coffee here before going on to the market?' Cesar indicated an empty table that had appeared in one of those cafés.

'Yes, please.' Grace sat down slowly, unable to stop looking at the sights and listening to the sounds around her. 'This is just amazing! Incredible!'

Cesar chuckled softly as he lowered his length down in the chair opposite. 'If memory serves me correctly, you will find that your retina will continue to be assaulted by the brightness of the colours long after we have returned to the apartment.'

Grace gave him a smile of acknowledgement as she continued to enjoy the loud conversation and laughter of the other patrons as they drank coffee or beer with their lunch as Cesar gave the waiter their order.

'With your agreement we will have lunch at Plaza Dorrego. It is where they hold the market at weekends,' Cesar supplied at her questioning look.

'And what happens there during the week?'

He shrugged. 'The cafés and restaurants supply tables for people to play cards or chess, and many others either watch or dance the tango.'

She gave a slow and wondrous shake of her head. 'How do you ever manage to drag yourself away from such a beautiful and vibrant city, even on business?'

Cesar smiled as he relaxed back in his chair. 'In the full knowledge that I will always come back.'

Grace nodded slowly. 'Of course.'

'You feel the same way about London, no doubt?'

'Yes and no,' she answered after a few seconds' consideration. 'I really fell in love with Paris when I was living there. Beth is back in London now, of course, after going to uni in Oxford for four years, but still it doesn't feel quite so much like home since my parents both died.'

'You miss them very much.' It was a statement rather than a question.

Grace nodded. 'Dad died four years ago, but it's only been a couple of months since Mum died,' she said wistfully. 'She was very ill for several months, and it was really hard, just watching her fade away.'

Cesar sat forward to place his hand over one of hers as it rested on the tabletop. 'You should have no regrets, Grace; I am sure you did everything you could to make life more comfortable for her at the end.'

Her eyes had misted over with tears. 'Unfortunately that doesn't make losing her any easier to bear.'

Cesar's fingers tightened briefly about hers before releasing them as the waiter arrived with their coffees.

He sat back, lids lowered, as he continued to watch Grace's enjoyment of their surroundings as she slowly sipped her coffee. She was, he had discovered these past few days, a woman who was as beautiful on the inside as she was on the outside. A woman who cared for her family, without regard for herself. Who empathised with others, also without regard for herself. As she had empathised with both his parents and himself at the devastating toll taken on them all over their loss of Gabriela.

Cesar had thought long and hard the previous night about Grace's comments after Raphael had left him. Admittedly she had been angry when she made them, but that did not make them any less the truth.

Most especially her accusation that Cesar had shut himself away in an ivory tower, totally removed from people and the world about him. It was one way of coping with the pain, of course. But, as Grace had also pointed out so succinctly, it was an ivory tower that effectively kept other people out, rather than just protecting Cesar and his family.

People like the young couple at the next table, who had eyes only for each other. Like the three old men sitting on a bench a short distance away, as they enjoyed discussing and settling the problems of the world, in the way that only the older generation could. Or the mother walking by with her two young children, all of them happily eating ice cream and talking excitedly. Or the gaggle of teenage boys, rolling past on battered skateboards.

All of them as vulnerable, in their own way, as Cesar and his family had been twenty-one years ago. But all continuing to live their lives, enjoying those lives, rather than shutting themselves away for fear of what might or might not happen to them now, or some time in the distant future. Because they all knew something Cesar had forgotten, something that Grace had now helped him to realize: that life couldn't be lived that way, that it wasn't living at all to be shut away in an ivory tower, no matter how comfortable it might be.

It was time for Cesar to leave his ivory tower, to shake off the restrictions he had placed about his life. And what better place to do that than the vibrant and beautiful city of Buenos Aires!

With the equally beautiful and vibrant Grace Blake.

CHAPTER NINE

'YOU CAN'T BE serious…?' Grace protested incredulously as Cesar took hold of her hand and pulled her forwards with the obvious intention of accepting the invitation for members of the watching crowd to now participate and join the couples of street performers in dancing the tango.

They had left the brightly painted area where they had lingered over drinking their coffee some time ago, and walked the short distance to the Plaza Dorrego and the market. Grace had thoroughly enjoyed herself as they strolled amongst the market stalls looking at antiques and other memorabilia, most of it totally impractical for taking back home as a present for Beth. She had finally settled on a soft brown leather jacket the same colour as Beth's eyes, and which would look lovely against her sister's blonde hair, more than happy to allow Cesar to handle the haggling over the price, something the market vendors seemed to expect and appreciate if the smiles on their faces were any indication.

Lunch had been a delicious salad eaten at one of the tables outside a busy restaurant in the cobbled square, after which they had wandered over to watch the professional street performers, three couples, all dancing the tango brilliantly, and accompanied by several equally accomplished musicians.

That Cesar was now considering—insisting—that the two of them participate was totally unbelievable.

'You said that you danced the tango,' he reminded her as he pulled her into the roped off area with several other couples who had also decided to accept the invitation.

'I believe what I actually said was that I danced it badly, and that Beth is much better at it than I am.' Grace looked about them uncomfortably as the watching crowd began to clap in expectation.

'Beth is not here,' Cesar drawled as he slipped off his leather jacket, revealing the muscled width of his shoulders in the black tee shirt as he reached out pointedly for her jacket and bags.

'And even if she were I doubt you would persuade her into a public display, either!' Grace looked up at him pleadingly.

'Time to smell the roses, Grace,' Cesar drawled, dark eyes challenging.

Her mouth firmed as he returned yesterday's comment at her. 'I'm really not that good.'

He gave a grin. 'But I am.'

Grace's eyes widened. 'You're very confident.'

He raised dark brows. 'Perhaps you would like to put that confidence to the test?'

'As it happens—yes!' She straightened to give him her two bags, before slipping her own jacket from her shoulders and handing that to him too.

Cesar moved to place them on the ground beside the musicians before rejoining Grace on the makeshift dance floor. 'Care to assume the position?'

'Ooh, you really are full of it today, aren't you?' She gave a reproving shake of her head as she moved into his arms.

'You have no idea.' Once again he threw one of her

own comments back at her. 'Just keep looking into my eyes and follow my lead,' he instructed huskily, holding her flush against his upper torso with just one arm about her back, his other arm behind his back, as the musicians began to play.

If someone had told Grace just a few days ago, when she had first met the arrogantly remote Cesar Navarro, what was going to happen next, then she wouldn't have believed them.

It was impossible to do anything but follow as Cesar effortlessly guided her through a series of complicated steps, gracefully, and in perfect time to the music. And as he did so he continued to hold Grace so tightly her breasts were pressed against his muscled chest, their gazes locked, Grace finding it impossible to look away from captivating deep brown eyes. Deep brown eyes that flashed with the fire and passion of the dance.

It was at once the most thrilling and arousing experience of Grace's life!

So much so that by the end of the dance she was moving just as effortlessly as Cesar, moving her feet in perfect synchronisation with his, and she was laughing up into his face only inches from her own, her hand placed dramatically against his cheek, when he bent her back over his arm as the music came to an end.

Which was when she heard the sound of thunderous applause and she turned her head sideways to find that everyone else had stopped dancing some time ago, even the professional street performers, so that they might stand back and watch her and Cesar dance.

Cesar seemed totally unaffected by all the attention as he continued to hold her draped over his arm. 'Well?' he asked softly, not even appearing to be breathing hard from their exertions.

'You win,' Grace breathed, her face flushed—and not just from the attention they were now receiving. 'You really do know how to dance the tango!'

The tango was, and always had been, one of the most sensuous dances to perform—which was probably why Grace had never got the hang of it before today; she had always been given a spotty-faced teenager as her partner during dance classes—and Cesar, as he had claimed, was very good at it. So much so that dancing with him had become a highly erotic experience; their movements had been graceful and yet highly sensual, to a degree that Grace's pulse was now pounding and her breasts were aroused, the nipples hard and swollen against Cesar's chest.

'Time to take a bow and make our escape, do you think?' Cesar murmured softly.

'Yes, please,' Grace answered huskily.

He straightened before twirling her to his side with a flourish as they both took a much-deserved bow, laughingly refusing the professional dancers' invitation—the three beautiful women especially pouting their disappointment as they looked at Cesar admiringly!—for them to dance again, the two of them finally able to make their escape a few minutes later.

'The apartment and siesta? Or do you wish to see some more of Buenos Aires first?' Cesar prompted softly as he helped Grace back into her jacket, his hands lingering on her shoulders once he had performed the deed.

'The apartment, if that's okay with you?' she answered huskily, very aware of his close proximity, all of her senses seeming sharper, heightened, after the exhilaration of the dance.

'And siesta?'

Grace glanced back over her shoulder at Cesar, the sensual languor in the darkness of his eyes unmistakeable. 'And siesta,' she echoed.

It seemed the most natural thing in the world for the two of them to walk along hand in hand as they strolled back to the apartment, Grace totally aware of Cesar as he moved along beside her with that animal grace that was such a natural part of him, a finger linked through the loop in the jacket slung over his shoulder, and revealing that muscled torso in the black fitted tee shirt and the jeans low down on the leanness of his hips.

Nor did Grace miss the covetous glances given his way by every woman they passed, young and old, accompanied or alone, as they obviously appreciated all that masculine beauty.

Also appreciated all that masculine beauty, Grace acknowledged ruefully—because she was so aware of Cesar now, so attuned to his easy sensuality of movement, that she could barely breathe, her breasts still highly sensitive inside the lace cups of her bra, the snug fit of her jeans heightening the arousal between her thighs.

Cesar seemed totally unaffected by the covetous glances being sent his way as he turned to smile at Grace often, a slow and sensuous smile that set her pulse racing in anticipation of the promised 'siesta'.

'Thank you so much for taking me out today and showing me your beautiful city,' Grace said as the two of them travelled up to the apartment in the lift together.

He looked at her beneath hooded lids, easily noting the flush to her cheeks and the brightness of her eyes, her lips full and pouting and slightly parted. Kissably so. 'The day does not have to end just yet, Grace,' he murmured softly.

She caught her breath sharply. 'I'm really not sure this is a good idea…'

Cesar turned so that his body was flush against hers, his hands resting on the mirrored wall either side of her head, the darkness of his gaze easily holding hers captive. 'Did you enjoy dancing with me today, Grace?' he prompted huskily.

She breathed shallowly. 'It was…wonderful.'

He nodded, ignoring the fact that the lift had now come to a halt and the doors opened. 'As I enjoyed dancing with you. But we both know it was more than that.'

Yes, it had been more than that. Dancing an erotically charged dance like the tango, with a man like Cesar, was almost akin to making love to music!

Grace moistened her lips with the tip of her tongue, her eyes widening as she saw Cesar's gaze following that sensuous movement. 'It could be a mistake on our part to take this any further—' She broke off as Cesar chuckled ruefully. 'What's so funny?' she demanded.

Cesar gave a shake of his head. 'Have you not heard it said that dancing is merely a prelude to a deeper intimacy?'

Her cheeks blazed with colour. 'I have, yes.'

His lids lowered. 'Then you cannot help but be aware of how much I desired you earlier, and how much I wish to make love to you now.'

'I— No,' she confirmed huskily.

'Or that you also wish for that deeper intimacy between us?'

Her throat moved as she swallowed. 'How can I deny it, when you must also know—be able to feel, how aroused I am?'

Yes, Cesar could feel Grace's arousal: the firm swell of her breasts tipped by engorged nipples, the heat of her thighs pressed against the long length of his own arousal. 'Just as you can feel my desire for you?'

'Yes.' Those two wings of colour deepened in her cheeks.

'Put your arms about my waist, Grace,' he encouraged gruffly.

Grace was trembling so badly—from Cesar's close proximity and the unmistakeable sexual tension sparking between them—that it was all she could do to lift her arms, that trembling increasing as she felt the warmth of Cesar's body through his tee shirt, his muscles flexing as she placed her hands against his back.

'What are you—?' she broke off her squeaked protest as Cesar's hands beneath her bottom lifted her up and into him, her legs moving instinctively about his waist as she now clung to the muscled broadness of his shoulders.

'Cesar?' She looked up at him as he stepped out of the lift with her still in his arms.

The darkness of his gaze almost seemed to sear her it was so hot. 'Your bedroom or mine?'

Grace's heart gave a leap in her chest. 'I—'

'Your bedroom or mine?' Cesar repeated tautly, a nerve pulsing in his clenched jaw.

She looked at him wordlessly for several seconds, those flames leaping even higher in the dark depths of his eyes. 'Yours,' she finally breathed softly; she hadn't seen Cesar's bedroom as yet, and a part of her was still able to rationalise—barely!—that it might be easier for her if she wanted to leave Cesar's bedroom later than to persuade him into leaving her own bedroom.

'Good choice.' He gave a tense smile, his expression just as intense as he strode down the hallway still carrying Grace in his arms.

Grace rested her head against his shoulder, relieved not to meet anyone on that walk down the hallway, not Maria, not Raphael, or any of his men, and she laughed breathlessly as Cesar kicked his bedroom door closed behind them before slowly lowering her onto her feet. Grace dropped her bags on the carpeted floor, her arms going up over Cesar's shoulders as he pressed her back against the door before lowering his head to claim her lips with his own.

Already aroused, by the dance earlier, strolling back to the apartment holding Cesar's hand, their time in the lift together, and being carried in Cesar's arms, the desire that had simmered beneath the surface until now exploded into a wild and heated burst of passion.

The two of them kissed hungrily, deeply, long and heated kisses, as their hands roamed in restless caresses, Grace's up and down the length of Cesar's spine, one of his hands moving to cup beneath the weight of her aroused and swollen breast as he plucked the hard peak of her nipple, their ragged breathing and throaty groans the only sounds in the silence of the bedroom.

Cesar's other hand became entangled in the long length of her hair as his lips moved from hers down the length of her arched throat, the hand that had cupped her breast now slowly unfastening the buttons at the front of her blouse, and he pushed the material down her arms before unclipping her bra and disposing of that, too.

'You are so beautiful here, Grace.' His lips moved down to the slope of her bared breasts. 'So very, very beautiful!' He captured one roused and turgid nipple into the moist heat of his mouth even as his hand cupped beneath her other breast to pluck the roused berry in the same rhythm as he suckled its twin deeply, hungrily.

Grace moved restlessly against him, her hands becoming entangled in the dark thickness of his hair as pleasure throbbed hotly, moistly, between her heated thighs. She wrapped one of her legs about his thighs as she rubbed that throbbing ache against and along the length of his shaft, needing, hungering for the release building higher and higher inside her.

She gasped out loud as Cesar cupped between her thighs, the soft pad of his thumb instinctively finding the throbbing nubbin and caressing, pressing, to the same rhythm as he suckled her nipple harder and deeper into the heat of his mouth, tongue lathing, teeth gently nipping at that sensitised berry before he bit down harder still, Cesar's arm moving about her in support as Grace's knees gave way as the pleasure of her release washed over and through her, consuming her.

Cesar continued to hold her, caress her, his tongue lathing, teeth gently biting, prolonging Grace's pleasure until she collapsed against his chest from the intensity of a release that left her weak and gasping.

'I want you. Now!' he rasped urgently as he swung Grace up into his arms and carried her across the room, laying her down on the bed before joining her on top of the deep green bedspread.

'Could I—? May I touch you first?'

'If you wish.'

'I do,' Grace murmured, uncaring of the nakedness of her breasts as she moved up to gently push Cesar back against the pillows. He looked so unlike himself, dark hair messily tousled from her caressing fingers, eyes burning with a dark intensity, a flush to his high cheekbones, lips parted as he breathed raggedly.

That raggedness increased as Grace slowly pushed his tee shirt up over the defined flatness of his abdomen and muscled chest, her gaze holding his as she lowered her head to taste that bronzed flesh with her lips and tongue.

Grace hummed low in her throat as his fingers became entangled in the long length of her hair, holding her to him as she tasted and licked that hot male flesh, lips lingering against one of the dark brown nubbins nestled amongst the darkness of his chest hair. She heard Cesar's gasp, his back arching as her tongue flicked across his sensitised flesh before she suckled him in the same way he had suckled her just minutes ago.

'Lower, Grace!'

'Lower?' she voiced uncertainly.

'If you please,' he encouraged gruffly.

Grace moved to kneel between his legs to kiss her way down his abdomen, following the dark V of hair to the waistband of his jeans, looking up at him uncertainly before flicking open the four buttons and tugging the heavy material down to his thighs, black boxers now the only covering to the long length of his arousal.

'Those, too, Grace!' he encouraged throatily.

She swallowed before peeling the boxers down to his thighs, too, her eyes widening as she released him fully to her hungry gaze. Cesar was beautiful. Absolutely beautiful. Nine inches of long, thick arousal that surged hotly against her hand as Grace reached out to touch him tentatively.

'Hold me, Grace,' he urged hotly.

She wrapped her fingers about that thickened shaft, instantly enthralled by the way the pulsing hardness leapt in response to her caress, and creamy liquid escaped the slitted tip.

'Lick me, Grace,' Cesar groaned. '*Madre mia*, take me in your mouth and lick me! Unless you would rather not?'

'Teach me—tell me how to please you,' Grace encouraged, her caresses becoming more daring as she followed Cesar's hoarse instructions and felt and saw his uninhibited response.

'Oh, yes!' Cesar hissed as he felt the heat of Grace's

lips and tongue, as she first licked his length from his balls to the bulbous tip, lingering over that sensitive spot just beneath the head, before moving up and over him as she first licked up the escape of fluid from the tip before taking him fully into the heat of her mouth.

Cesar's back arched even as his fingers tightened in the long length of Grace's hair, holding her to him, over him, as his hips instinctively thrust up into the heat of her mouth, her tongue now a moist rasp across and around that swollen and sensitised head as she eagerly lapped up his escaping juices, all the time her fingers gently pumping.

'Like that, yes!' It was both exquisite pleasure and exquisite torture as Grace's other hand now cupped beneath his sac, gently squeezing, as she continued to suck and lick the throbbing tip into the heat of her mouth in the same rhythm as her fingers pumped and caressed.

Over and over again, round and round, those fingers pumping up and down, Cesar no longer needing to encourage her as the pleasure she gave him became all that mattered, all that Cesar knew, his sac tightening as that pleasure reached an unbearable pitch.

'You have to stop now, Grace.' He groaned low and long as she experimented and sucked him deep to the back of her throat. 'I am going to— I do not think— Grace…!' Cesar gave up all hope of maintaining control as he felt the lava-like heat of his release course down the length of his shaft before exploding into the welcoming, lapping warmth of Grace's mouth. Pulsing, releasing, again and again, Cesar's breathing a harsh rasp in the silence as he continued to thrust mindlessly to the back of her throat until he knew he was completely spent. 'Oh, God, Grace, I did not mean— I should not have— I have more control than to— Correction, I usually have more control,' he amended. 'Are you all right?'

She sat back to smile down at him shyly. 'Are you?'

'Very much so. But I—I did not hurt you?' He looked up at her with concern.

'Of course not. Did I hurt you?' Her cheeks coloured prettily.

'You may "hurt" me like that again any time. What the—?' Cesar broke off with a muttered expletive in his own language as a knock sounded on his bedroom door.

'Grace?' He looked up at her regretfully as she moved back sharply, her face paling as she turned to look at the door. 'Grace—'

'You should get that,' she muttered awkwardly as another knock sounded on the door, scrambling over to the side of the bed before standing up jerkily to quickly gather up her blouse and holding it in front of her bared breasts as she turned away.

Cesar scowled darkly as he sat up to adjust his own clothing, before standing up to refasten his denims. 'Grace.'

'Not now, Cesar.' She stepped back to avoid his touch as he reached out for her, her gaze now lowered uncomfortably to the carpeted floor.

'But—'

'I am sorry to interrupt, Cesar.' Raphael's voice came urgently through the closed bedroom door. 'But I must to speak with you immediately!'

Cesar gave Grace one last regretful glance before crossing the room to wrench open the bedroom door, knowing by the way Raphael's gaze moved briefly over Cesar's dishevelled appearance, before shifting behind him to the ruffled bed—and possibly Grace herself?—that the other man was aware of at least some of what had just taken place in the bedroom. 'This had better be good, Raphael,' he warned in a low and dangerous voice.

Grace took advantage of Cesar filling the bedroom doorway to quickly pull on her blouse and refasten it. She had no hope of understanding the two men's conversation as they spoke rapidly in Spanish, but she could see Cesar's profile and saw the way the colour drained from his cheeks.

Whatever Raphael was telling him so urgently it wasn't welcome news…

CHAPTER TEN

'I HAVE TO GO, Grace!' Cesar turned to her as Raphael left, his face a sickly grey colour, his eyes pained. 'There has been an accident. My parents. On the way to the airport earlier. Raphael has been trying to locate me for the past two hours.'

'No!' Grace breathed shakily as she reached out to the edge of the bed for support.

'They are both still alive,' Cesar assured her grimly. 'My father received only superficial wounds, but Mama suffered a head injury and is still unconscious. I have to go to the hospital immediately, to be with them.'

'Of course you do,' she accepted softly.

'You will come with me? A woman's presence may be appreciated,' he added gruffly as Grace gave him a startled glance.

'Of course I'll come to the hospital with you if you want me to,' she assured him quickly, having no idea what she could do to aid the two strong Navarro men, but certainly willing to accompany Cesar if he wanted her with him.

'What I want is for this not to have happened at all, and for the two of us to still be—' Cesar broke off with an impatient shake of his head. 'Can you be ready to leave in five minutes?'

'Of course.' Grace desperately needed to go to the privacy of her own bedroom and tidy her appearance and brush her tangled hair!

No, she really couldn't go there now, she instructed herself firmly. Or think of the fact that she was the one responsible for Cesar not having his security guards or mobile phone with him today. And that when his parents' car had crashed the two of them were probably dancing the tango together. That when his mother lay unconscious in hospital the two of them had returned to the apartment undetected—because the security cameras were switched off!—and gone to Cesar's bedroom to make love together.

No, she wouldn't think of any of that now. Perhaps later, once Cesar's mother was conscious and they had all been reassured of her complete recovery. Then Grace could indulge in all the self-recriminations she wanted.

As Cesar would eventually no doubt also realise that, but for Grace and her phobia about the security he surrounded himself with day and night, he would have known of his parents accident much earlier...

'I'm so sorry, Raphael.' Grace winced as she looked up at the stony-faced man leaning back against the corridor wall outside the hospital room into which Cesar had minutes ago disappeared to be beside his father at his mother's bedside.

'It's my fault, because I was so angry over being seen on those security cameras last night, that Cesar left his mobile phone in the apartment and refused his security today.' She gave a shake of her head as she recalled how much she had hated the thought of facing Raphael again after what he had witnessed on the security footage last night; in light of what had happened today that embarrassment now seemed totally irrelevant.

'Cesar is a grown man who is perfectly capable of making his own decisions,' Raphael cut in frostily.

'But—'

'While your guilt is admirable, Grace, at this moment it is also misplaced,' he added dismissively. 'The omission of Cesar's security and mobile phone did not cause the tyre to burst on Mr Navarro's car, causing him to lose control of the vehicle and crash into a wall.'

'But if you had been able to contact Cesar he would at least have been at the hospital earlier—'

'Perhaps,' he allowed grimly. 'But whether Cesar was here or not would not have changed the fact that Esther Navarro has not regained consciousness since the accident.'

Grace gave a pained frown. 'You're really very angry but hiding it well, aren't you?'

He bared his teeth in the semblance of a smile. 'Yes.'

Grace chewed on her bottom lip. 'I really am very sorry. I didn't think—'

'Grace, I was a soldier for many years, and as a soldier I have been trained to deal with what is, not what might have or should have been. Cesar was unreachable for over four hours today, and that is, indeed, regrettable,' he bit out tautly, 'but it is not relevant to the situation that exists now.'

No, it wasn't. And Grace was just expressing her own guilt rather than dealing with the situation that existed now; Cesar was all that mattered now, and the return to consciousness of his mother.

'You're right.' Grace straightened determinedly. 'You can tell me what you truly think of me later. Right now it's Cesar and his parents who are important.'

Raphael gave an abrupt inclination of his head. 'In that, at least, we are agreed.'

She chewed her bottom lips again. 'Cesar told me that

the two of you were at school together, and have remained friends ever since?'

He glanced towards the closed hospital room door. 'Did he?'

Grace sensed that Raphael wasn't too pleased at being the subject of one of their conversations. 'He wasn't breaking a confidence or anything, and only told me that much because I'd thought that the two of you were—' She broke off as she realised she was just digging a bigger hole for herself, her concern for Esther Navarro causing her to babble.

Raphael arched dark brows over piercing blue eyes. 'The two of us were what?'

She felt the colour warm her cheeks. 'Well, the two of you are always together, and at the time I made the comment I hadn't realised that you were his personal security guard, and so I thought—assumed—wrongly, as it happens—'

'That Cesar and I are…?'

Grace gave another pained grimace at the dangerous softness of Raphael's tone. 'Involved.'

He continued to look down at her wordlessly for several long seconds, any number of thoughts going through his head—and none of them in the least readable from the blandness of his expression! 'You know, Grace,' he finally spoke softly, 'for a woman who, for the past ten minutes or so, has been poised delicately on the edge of remaining standing in this corridor or being hurled out of a third-floor hospital window, you are continuing to display a remarkable lack of self-preservation!'

She winced. 'The third-floor window is winning out at the moment, hmm?'

'Undoubtedly.' He nodded tersely. 'But I am beginning to understand why Cesar is intrigued by you.'

Her eyes widened. 'You are?'

Raphael nodded curtly. 'Your conversation is very forthright, something I do not believe has happened to Cesar often—if ever before.'

Grace gave a rueful smile. 'But something he can live without, I'm sure.'

Raphael returned her smile. 'Perhaps. But—' He broke off as the door across the corridor opened suddenly, Cesar looming in the doorway.

Cesar's lids narrowed as he took in the fact that Grace, the woman he had recently made love with, and Raphael, the man who was his closest friend and his Head of Security, appeared to be talking softly together and sharing a companionable smile. His gaze turned flinty as it levelled on Grace. 'Would you mind sitting with my father for a few minutes while I go and talk with the doctor about my mother's condition?'

'I— No, of course I don't mind.' She straightened awkwardly before slipping past him into the hospital room.

Cesar raised questioning brows at his oldest friend. 'Do you not have somewhere else you need to be?'

The other man was completely unaffected by the coldness of Cesar's tone as he gave a dismissive shrug. 'As your Head of Security, you are my primary concern, and after today where you go I go.'

Cesar's mouth thinned. 'You—'

'Cesar.' Raphael spoke softly but firmly. 'You are not in a good place right now, and so not thinking logically, but once you are you will realise that I have absolutely no personal interest in your Grace Blake!'

He stiffened. 'She is not my Grace Blake—'

'No?'

'No,' Cesar rasped.

The other man shrugged. 'Shall we find your mother's doctor?'

Cesar drew in a sharp breath at this timely reminder of the reason he had left his mother's bedside, even briefly. 'I will apologise for my remarks later.'

'Take it as said,' Raphael dismissed as the two of them strode off down the corridor in the direction of the nurses' station.

If Grace had needed any further proof of Carlos Navarro's continuing love for his estranged wife, then she had it the moment she walked into Esther Navarro's hospital room and saw that he appeared to have aged twenty years since she had seen him the evening before; his face, so much like Cesar's, was pale and all sharp hollows beneath his cut and grazed swarthy skin, his eyes dark wells of pain as he gazed down at his unconscious wife and gently held one of her lifeless hands in both of his. Even those distinguished wings of grey at his temples seemed more plentiful in the darkness of his tousled hair.

Grace quietly moved to sit in the chair drawn up beside the bed on the opposite side, where Cesar had obviously so recently sat, not speaking, but hoping to silently give Carlos Navarro strength and comfort by her presence.

Esther Navarro lay pale and still against the white bed sheets, blonde hair splayed out against the pillows, her beautiful face unmarked but for the bruised bump visible on her left temple, and the obvious reason for her lack of consciousness.

Grace instinctively reached out and clasped Esther's other hand in her own, surprised at how cold it was. If anything should happen to Cesar's beloved mother...!

But it wouldn't. It couldn't! Hadn't the Navarro family already suffered enough when they lost Gabriela, without—?

'I loved her from the moment I set eyes on her.' Carlos Navarro's voice sounded somehow rusty and unused in the midst of the bleeps and soft murmur of the machines monitoring his wife's vital signs, the darkness of his ravaged gaze not leaving the pale beauty of her face.

Grace, not even sure that Carlos knew it was her sitting opposite him, rather than Cesar, wisely remained silent, knowing that Carlos needed to talk, and that it didn't really matter who he talked to, only that he did so. Although the fact that he spoke in English seemed to imply that, on some level at least, he was aware of Grace's presence...

'She was hiking through Argentina as part of a year of travelling before attending college.' He continued to talk softly. 'A tall Amazon of a woman with the longest, silkiest blonde hair I had ever seen, sitting outside a café in San Telmo drinking coffee, as I chanced to walk by on my way to a business meeting. I never did make it to the meeting, but instead asked Esther if I might join her for coffee.' He smiled wistfully at the memory. 'It was love at first sight, for both of us, and we were never apart after that first meeting, were married within the month. Cesar was born exactly nine months later, and so Esther never did go to college.' He gave a wistful smile. 'I still remember the way she looked the day Cesar was born, a Madonna with child. My beautiful blonde-haired angel. So like our little—' He came to an abrupt halt as his voice broke emotionally. 'Twenty-one years, Miss Blake.' His eyes were dark pits of torment as he looked across the bed at Grace. 'I lost my angel the day our daughter was taken from us, and now—now—'

'Esther will recover, Mr Navarro. I know she will.' Grace spoke firmly, with certainty, totally convinced that the fates couldn't be so cruel, to Carlos or Cesar, as to take their beloved Esther from them after all they had already lost.

'Thank you!' he breathed raggedly.

'You have to believe she will wake up.' And when she did, Grace sincerely hoped that Esther and Carlos would be able to sort out their differences, once and for all; the love glowing in Carlos Navarro's eyes as he gazed down at his wife told her he didn't deserve to live without his angel for even a day longer.

'I obviously will not be returning to England today, as I originally intended.' Cesar looked down into Grace's pale face where she had briefly joined him in the hospital corridor outside his mother's room, Esther having finally regained consciousness, the doctor having assured them there was no brain damage, that after a day's rest she would be none the worse for the experience apart from a bruise on her temple. They did, however, wish to keep Esther under observation for at least some of that time. Time Cesar intended to remain here and support his mother and his father. 'But that is no reason that I cannot arrange for the jet to fly you back to England later this evening, if that is what you wish?' He waited tensely for Grace's answer.

She looked up at him searchingly. 'What would you like me to do?'

A good question. But not one Cesar had a straightforward answer to. A part of him dearly wanted Grace to say she would stay in Argentina for as long as her presence might be of help to him or his parents. The other half of him was aware that the two of them had stepped over a line earlier today.

Cesar loved his parents, and his friendship with Raphael was one of mutual respect and affection, but, other than those ties of family and friendship, Cesar did not allow anyone to pierce the barrier he had placed over his emotions after Gabriela was taken from them. Grace Blake had breached that barrier. To what extent, Cesar did not yet know. And until he did, it would perhaps be better if she were to return to England.

'Never mind.' Grace spoke flatly, Cesar's continued silence answer enough. 'Perhaps, if it's not too much trouble, you could ask Raphael to arrange for the plane to fly me back to England today?'

'If that is what you wish.' He nodded stiffly.

What Grace wished was that none of the past few hours had happened!

Certainly not the Navarros' car crash. But also Cesar switching off the security cameras in his apartment. Leaving his mobile behind when they went out without his bodyguard. Dancing the tango together. Making love together in Cesar's bedroom.

Mostly she wished that the latter had never happened.

Even now, several hours later, and with Cesar back to being that coldly remote stranger Grace had first met, she found it difficult to meet his gaze. Found it difficult to look at him at all when she remembered the intimacies the two of them had shared such a short time ago.

Not that anyone looking at the two of them now would guess they had ever been intimate; Cesar was once again the arrogantly remote Cesar Navarro, and Grace—well, the last few hours had been so fraught with tension, of one kind or another, that she barely knew who she was any more, let alone what to make of her behaviour earlier in Cesar's bedroom.

Certainly she had never indulged in such intimacies with another man before today. Before Cesar. Intimacies that made her blush just to think of them. Which was why

Grace had been trying so hard, these past two hours of waiting around at the hospital, to put them from her mind. There would be plenty of time, both for soul-searching, and recriminations, once she was alone on the plane taking her back to England.

She raised her chin as her gaze focused on Cesar's tee-shirt-covered chest rather than his face. 'It is,' she said firmly.

He nodded tersely. 'I will have Raphael drive you back to the apartment.'

'There's no need for that.' Her gaze flickered up to Cesar's face, and then as quickly away again, just that one glance at the coldness of his expression and chill in his glittering gaze enough to tell her that the two of them had nothing to say to each other. 'I can easily get a taxi—'

'I said Raphael will drive you,' Cesar rasped harshly.

And the two of them were obviously back to a situation where what Cesar said was going to happen was exactly what happened. 'If you insist.'

'I do, yes.' The coldness of his tone brooked no further argument.

'Grace, I— We will talk further when I am able to return to England.'

She tensed. 'Talk about what?'

'Do not be naïve, Grace,' he bit out tersely. 'We obviously need to discuss what happened earlier today.'

'I don't see why.' She forced herself to look up and meet that coldly glittering gaze. 'You're going to remain in Argentina for several more days, and I shall be leaving your employment soon anyway—unless you would prefer me to already have gone before you return to England?' she added uncertainly. That alternative would certainly save them both the embarrassment of having to see each other again.

'Of course I do not wish you to—!' Cesar broke off his angry reply to draw in several deep and controlling breaths before speaking again. 'By all means take the time of my absence to perhaps visit with your sister in London, but you will certainly remain in my employment until we have had chance to speak again.'

Just the thought of being with the light-hearted Beth for a few days, away from the tensions of being anywhere near Cesar, was enough to lift Grace's spirits. Even just the thought of that talk Cesar wanted once he had returned to England filled her with dread.

They really had completely overstepped the line between employer and employee earlier today. Irrevocably. To such an extent that Grace knew there was no going back. To a degree she knew she wouldn't be able to work out her three weeks' notice once Cesar was back in England, something he must also be aware of.

'Very well,' she accepted stiffly. 'If you wouldn't mind making those arrangements with Raphael, I'll go back to the apartment and pack my things.'

'Grace.'

'Yes?' She looked up at him warily.

Cesar drew in a sharp breath. Their relaxation during their sightseeing trip, dancing the tango together, and returning to the apartment to make love, seemed as if it had happened days ago rather than hours. Nor, at this point, did Cesar have any idea how he was going to feel, what he was going to say to Grace, when he returned to England and the two of them did have the opportunity to talk privately.

'Nothing,' he bit out tersely. 'I hope that you have an uneventful flight back to England.'

'Uneventful?' she echoed wryly.

Cesar's hands clenched at his sides. 'Grace, I am trying to maintain a politeness between us—'

'Why?'

He frowned as Grace looked up at him quizzically. 'It is for the best.'

'Perhaps,' she allowed with a grimace. 'Is there anything you want me to do once I'm back in England?'

'Such as?'

'I have no idea.' She sighed. 'I was merely returning your own politeness.'

And Cesar found her politeness as irritating as Grace probably had his own pitiable attempt! 'There are some papers for Raphael to collect from my study, but other than that I can think of nothing else that I will need.'

Nothing else that he needed…

Cesar certainly didn't need her, would never need her, Grace acknowledged heavily a short time later as she sat silent and withdrawn in the back of the car as Raphael drove her back to Cesar's apartment.

It was only as she was packing her things that Grace realised that the bra that matched the panties she was wearing was still in Cesar's bedroom somewhere. She had no intention of leaving it there for him to find when he returned home later today!

'What are you doing?'

Grace looked up guiltily from where she was kneeling on the carpeted floor searching for her bra beneath Cesar's bed, colour burning her cheeks as she saw the way in which Raphael's brows were raised in mocking query as he stood in the bedroom doorway looking across at her.

She sat back on her heels. 'I—er—I left something in here earlier.'

He folded his arms across the width of his chest. '"Something"?'

'Yes, I—ah.' Grace had finally located her bra hidden beneath the bedspread as it draped over the end of the bed, quickly picking it up to stuff it into her jeans pocket before standing up. 'What time are we—? Damn!' she muttered as she caught her elbow on a photo frame on the dressing table as she walked past, only just managing to catch it before it fell to the floor. 'I am such a—' She stopped dead as she looked down at the photograph she now held in her hand.

It was a photograph of Cesar, aged about eleven or twelve, with a little girl standing beside him and looking up at him adoringly, her tiny hand tucked trustingly into his much larger one.

A little blonde-haired angel, with deep brown eyes and a dimpled smile. His sister, Gabriela?

His sister, Gabriela, who looked all too familiar to Grace…

CHAPTER ELEVEN

'WHAT EXACTLY ARE you looking for, Grace...?' Beth watched curiously as Grace searched through the cupboards beneath the dresser in the kitchen they had shared with their parents for most of their lives.

It was almost twenty-four hours since Grace had knocked over that photograph in Cesar's bedroom in Buenos Aires. Twenty-four hours during which she had flown silently back to England with Raphael, before going to her bedroom to collect her things and then later driving up to London to see her sister. Twenty-four hours when Grace's emotions had fluctuated from being convinced she had to be wrong, to being absolutely sure that she wasn't.

What was she looking for now?

The impossible, surely?

Except, Grace couldn't be sure of that until she had found the photo album she was looking for. A photo album of Beth when she was younger. Much younger. A photo album that was all that Beth had left of the parents who had brought her up until she was five years old, when the Blakes had adopted her and she became Grace's younger sister.

Photographs that showed Beth as a brown-eyed blonde-haired angel...

The same brown-eyed blonde-haired angel standing

beside Cesar in the photograph displayed on his dressing table in his apartment in Buenos Aires?

Except it couldn't be.

Grace knew that it couldn't be.

And yet…

Until Grace found that old photo album, and looked at the photographs inside for herself, she simply couldn't dismiss the idea—the incredible, unbelievable idea—that Beth was somehow the missing Gabriela Navarro.

Grace had spent the whole of the flight back from Argentina unable to stop thinking of that photograph she had seen in Cesar's bedroom, wasting no time, once she had collected her things, in going to Cesar's study to say goodbye to Raphael, while at the same time checking as to whether the photograph on the desk was the same one in Cesar's bedroom in Buenos Aires, and not in the least surprised when she found that it was. Nor had she felt in the least guilty, when she had taken advantage of Raphael's distracted looking for Cesar's business papers, to have placed that second photograph quickly inside her shoulder bag and bring it up to London with her. Hopefully she would be able to put it back before Cesar returned from Argentina. She had needed to know, needed to compare—

'Ah ha!' Grace nodded her satisfaction as she finally pulled the old photo album out from beneath some more recent ones, holding it tightly to her chest as she slowly stood up.

'What on earth do you want with that?' Beth looked even more puzzled by her behaviour now.

'Probably nothing.' Grace frowned. 'Except— Let me just look at these photos first and then we'll talk.'

Beth looked totally bewildered. 'You've been acting very strangely since you got back, Grace. Did something happen in Buenos Aires that you want to talk about?'

A lot had happened in Buenos Aires—most of which Grace didn't want to talk about! Most especially she didn't want to talk about Cesar, or the fact that she thought she might have fallen in love with a man who was so far out of her league it would be funny if it weren't so heartbreaking!

Instead Grace found herself studying her sister—possibly as a way of delaying the moment when she had to look at the photographs in the album and compare them to the one she had secreted away in her shoulder bag.

Was the unusual blonde colour of Beth's hair, although longer in style, the exact same shade as Esther Navarro's?

Did Beth's chin have that same delicate curve as Esther's, too?

And were those brown eyes the same shape and rich dark brown as Carlos's and Cesar's?

Was it really possible that Beth might be the missing Gabriela Navarro, or was Grace just letting her imagination run away with her? Perhaps seeing a likeness where none existed? What did she know—maybe all blonde-haired two-year-olds looked alike, with their chubby little bodies and unformed features?

Besides which, a part of Grace didn't see how Beth could possibly be Gabriela Navarro, when she had been born in England, the only daughter of James and Carla Lawrence.

But another part of Grace couldn't deny the likeness between the young Gabriela Navarro and Beth. Nor could she dispel that nagging feeling of familiarity she had felt, but couldn't explain, when she was in Esther Navarro's company on Friday evening. Or that Cesar had mentioned his sister having been allergic to flower pollen, just as Beth was. Or the fact that Beth had always wished her 'sweet dreams' on their way to bed every night when they were children—and still did if they spoke on the telephone late at night!—in the same way that Cesar had in Buenos Aires, because his mother had always done that when he was a child. When Gabriela was a child, too…

All of them features of that muddled dream Grace had had a couple of nights ago.

And all of them maybe coincidences, but too much so for Grace to completely dismiss them as such until she had looked at Beth's childhood photographs again, and compared them to the one she now had of Cesar and his baby sister, Gabriela.

'You're creeping me out staring at me like that, you know.' Beth frowned across at her uncertainly.

'Sorry.' Grace gave a dismissive shake of her head. 'I was just— Never mind.' She smiled brightly. 'Just let me take a look at this and then I'll try to explain.' And she and Beth could either laugh together over Grace's wayward imaginings, or all hell was going to break loose!

'I should never have let you talk me into this,' Beth muttered uncomfortably as she sat beside Grace in a taxi on the way from their hotel to Cesar Navarro's Buenos Aires apartment, and looking very beautiful in the brown jacket that Grace had bought for her, that she'd teamed with a white tee shirt and black jeans.

Grace wasn't as confident about what she was doing as she appeared outwardly, either…

'And they weren't at all pleased with me at work for asking for this week's holiday so soon after I began working for them.' Beth frowned.

Grace reached out and gave her sister's hand a reassuring squeeze. 'You know why we're here, Beth.'

'Because you have totally lost your mind and somehow think I'm the long-lost Gabriela Navarro, yes,' her sister confirmed impatiently. 'And because I love you enough—

or I'm just stupid enough!—to have decided to indulge your fantasy!' she added crossly.

Yes, Grace still hadn't dismissed that 'hare-brained idea' that Beth might, just might, be Cesar's missing younger sister.

The photographs in Beth's album hadn't been conclusive, but the similarity between the two-year-old Gabriela Navarro, and Beth at the same age, had been close enough for Grace not to be able to dismiss her 'hare-brained idea', as Beth called it, that they were one and the same person.

The fact that there were no photographs of Beth before she was two had done nothing to dispel that belief...

The Lawrences' album was full of photos of Beth from the age of about two, dozens and dozens of them, but there wasn't a single photograph of her as a baby or as a one-year-old. The first photographs in that meticulously maintained album of Beth's childhood were of a fully formed toddler.

On the basis of that Grace had decided to explain the situation to Beth, before turning her attention to convincing her sister to take a week off work, and spending money they could ill afford on airfare, and flying back to Buenos Aires with her. If Grace was wrong, then she was wrong—and she obviously couldn't dismiss the knowledge that it would be a one-in-millions chance that she just happened to go and work for Cesar Navarro, and her own adopted sister looked exactly like his own missing sister! Just as she couldn't deny that fate could be a fickle thing... But surely it was better to know she was wrong, than to simply ignore all of Beth's similarities to Gabriela Navarro?

Grace thought so. She only hoped that Cesar would see it the same way, because if he didn't he was going to hate Grace for raising his hopes before perhaps having them completely dashed again when he proved that Beth couldn't possibly be his long-lost sister. To the point that he would never want to set eyes on either of the Blake sisters again!

Something which, having fallen in love with him, Grace was going to find unbearable. Not that she thought there was any future for the two of them anyway—how could there be, when they came from completely different worlds? But it was still going to be hard if Cesar coldly and completely dismissed her from his life. As he was sure to do if she was wrong about Beth being Gabriela…

Grace's heart was thundering in her chest, her palms damp as she paid off the taxi before she and Beth both turned to look up at the building where Cesar had his apartment. Grace was dressed very similarly to Beth in faded blue denims, with a white tee shirt beneath a black jacket. They looked, in fact, like any other two twenty-something women on holiday. Except this trip to Buenos Aires was no holiday…

'And you think I could be part of a family who live in places like this?' Beth gave a disbelieving snort at the obvious opulence of the apartment building.

'It's because I don't know that we have to do this, Beth,' Grace said nervously. 'You saw the photographs, the similarity between you and Gabriela Navarro, the fact that there were no baby photos of you—'

'And I also remember pointing out to you that there could just have been another, earlier album of me, as a baby, and it was lost or misplaced after my real parents died,' Beth reasoned dryly.

There could. Of course there could. And Grace had already thought of that possibility. It just wasn't enough of a possibility for her to completely dismiss the idea that Beth as a two-year-old had looked enough like Gabriela

Navarro to have been her twin. Or for her to actually be Gabriela Navarro.

The why and how that could even be possible were something Grace hadn't been able to confirm or deny, despite her efforts to do so in the two days before she and Beth flew out to Buenos Aires; the Lawrences had both been only children, with no parents or other family close enough to offer to look after five-year-old Beth after the couple had died. Or for Grace to question about Beth's very early childhood…

'Look on the bright side,' Grace encouraged her sister lightly. 'If nothing else you'll get to spend a week's holiday in Buenos Aires!'

Beth looked totally unconvinced. 'If the Navarros don't decide to have us arrested, or something equally nasty, for trying to practise a deception on them! I— This is— I must have been mad to have let you talk me into coming here!' She gave an impatient shake of her head as they entered the marble foyer of Cesar Navarro's apartment building. 'You do know that we're going to end up in jail for the week—or more?'

Grace sincerely hoped, whatever the outcome of this meeting with Cesar, that wouldn't be the case. And if it was, then so be it. Grace's employment with Cesar was going to end soon, anyway, after which she would never see him again, so she had nothing to lose if he should decide to terminate that employment immediately by throwing both her and Beth out of his apartment—and into jail! And, if her suspicions should turn out to be correct, then Cesar, and his family, had everything to gain.

Quite where that outcome would leave Grace in regard to Cesar was another matter.

Grace took a deep breath, before raising her hand to

press the intercom button that could—or would?—decide Beth's future, at least.

'Grace?' Cesar was frowning as he strode into the salon where Raphael had asked Grace to wait whilst he went to inform Cesar of her arrival.

'Hello, Cesar.' She stood up abruptly, her smile appearing nervous as she wiped her palms down denim-clad thighs.

'What are you doing here?' The darkness of his gaze remained fixed on her intently.

'I—I hope your mother has recovered completely now?' she prompted huskily.

Cesar nodded abruptly. 'She is still slightly fragile, but she is out of hospital, yes.'

'I'm so glad!' She gave another nervous smile.

Cesar, having thought he had several more days before he returned to England and talked with Grace, was now at a complete loss to know what to say until he knew why Grace had chosen to come back to Buenos Aires, especially when she must have flown on a public airline, using money he knew she could ill afford.

Cesar had put thoughts of Grace Blake, and that last day they had spent in Buenos Aires together, firmly to the back of his mind this past three days as he concentrated on his mother's recovery and father's obvious distress at believing he had almost lost Esther completely and for ever. Far easier, Cesar had decided, to lock Grace Blake away in a separate compartment of his emotions, one he could open and deal with once he returned to England.

And instead that closed compartment had now been ripped open by Grace's return to Buenos Aires. And he had no idea why she was here, did not dare to hope—

'I asked why you are here, Grace,' he repeated gruffly.

Her throat moved convulsively as she swallowed. 'I—er—I—'

'My sister thought I might enjoy a little holiday in Buenos Aires!' an unfamiliar voice cut in challengingly.

Cesar's gaze moved sharply to the young woman who had been standing in the shadowed alcove in front of one of the windows to his apartment, but now stepped out into the room. A tall and blonde-haired young woman, who had just proclaimed herself as being Grace's younger sister. 'Beth, is it not?' he said slowly.

'That's right.' She strode confidently across the room, her hand extended in greeting. 'It's a pleasure to meet you, Mr Navarro.'

Cesar made no move to take that hand as he instead stared down intently at the young woman who was only slighter shorter than he; not unexpectedly, there was absolutely no similarity between the two adopted sisters, either in height or colouring.

And yet Cesar felt a strange sense of familiarity…

'Mr Navarro?' Beth Blake quirked a questioning brow as he continued to ignore her hand.

'Who are you?' he rasped harshly.

Her hand dropped back to her side as she looked up at him quizzically. 'I just told you, I'm Grace's sister, Beth.'

Cesar turned to look at Grace. 'What exactly is going on, Grace?' he demanded coldly.

She moistened her lips with the tip of her tongue. 'I—'

'Is this your idea of joke?' Cesar continued as if she hadn't spoken, his eyes glittering darkly, hands clenched into fists at his side.

Not quite the reaction Grace had been hoping for!

Although it was obvious—and slightly heartening—to realise that Cesar could see the same similarities she could, between Beth and both his mother and his sister, Gabriela, in colouring at least. Just as obvious as it was that he was furiously angry with Grace for once again opening a wound he had spent years trying to heal. That he had definitely been starting to overcome that last carefree day Grace had spent with him in Buenos Aires…

Grace gave another swipe of her tongue across her lips. 'I— Before I left on Sunday I went to your bedroom to collect—something I had left there—' her cheeks blazed with colour '—and I saw the photograph of Gabriela and you on the dressing table—'

'His bedroom?' Beth was the one to repeat sharply. 'Grace, what were you doing in Cesar Navarro's bedro—?'

'Never mind that now,' Grace dismissed quickly, knowing that the sudden redness in her cheeks had to be evidence enough of why she had been in Cesar's bedroom four days ago. 'I saw the photograph, Cesar,' she continued firmly, 'and—well, surely you can see for yourself.' She waved a hand in Beth's general direction. 'The similarity is—'

'Purely cosmetic,' he cut in harshly, decisively. 'My sister is long gone, Grace, and this—' he also gave a wave of his hand in Beth's direction '—this is cruel and—'

'I should stop right there if I were you, buddy!' Beth poked a warning finger into his chest as she glared at him. 'My sister doesn't have a cruel bone in her body. She genuinely believes that I could somehow be related to you. Personally, having now met you, I'm rather grateful that I'm so obviously not,' she added disgustedly. 'But I assure you, Mr Navarro,' she continued as he narrowed his glittering gaze on her, 'that Grace is guilty of nothing more than a mistaken belief I might somehow be your long-lost little sister, Gabriela—'

'Gabriela?'

They all three turned to look at the tall blonde-haired

woman standing in the doorway, Grace with dismay, Cesar with barely contained fury, and Beth with—

Beth was staring at Esther Navarro as if she had seen a ghost.

Or a vision of herself as she might appear in thirty years' time?

Grace had had no idea that Esther would be at Cesar's apartment today, but, seeing Esther and Beth together for the first time, it was impossible not to note the similarities between the two women: the same unusual blonde hair—Esther's currently arranged in a style to best hide the purple bruising at her temple—the wide and creamy brow, the curve of their cheeks and determined chin, the fullness of their lips.

'Who are you?' Beth breathed shallowly.

Esther Navarro reached out for the support of the door-frame as she stumbled slightly, her eyes huge wells of blue in the paleness of her face as she continued to stare at Beth as if at an apparition. 'I believe that was to be my own next question…' she murmured faintly.

'You should not be out of bed, Mama.' Cesar strode forcefully across the room to his mother's side. 'Grace was just introducing her sister to me—'

'Grace's sister?' Esther turned to him with bewildered eyes. 'But surely, Cesar, you must see—'

'I see only a young woman with a passing resemblance to—to someone we once knew,' Cesar rasped with another coldly accusing glance at Grace. 'Let me help you back to your bedroom, Mama, and then I will come back and deal with this situation.'

Esther waved away the supportive arm he might have placed about her waist as she stepped further into the room. 'But…'

'Grace and her sister will be leaving as soon as—'

'Grace and her sister won't be going anywhere until they're good and ready, buddy,' Beth interrupted firmly. 'And I resent being referred to as a "situation".'

'You will cease calling me 'buddy' in that derogatory tone.'

'I'll call you anything I damn well please—buddy!' Beth glared back at Cesar with blazing blue eyes. 'Just what do you think gives you the right to talk about Grace and I as if we're something nasty that you've accidentally found on the bottom of one of your handmade leather shoes?'

Cesar straightened to his full height of well over six feet before striding across the room until he stood only inches away from Beth, his expression one of haughty arrogance as he looked down the length of his nose at her. 'You are in my home, and not as an invited guest, and as such I believe I am perfectly within my rights to talk to you in any way I choose.'

'That's what you think, buddy—'

'That is what I know!' Cesar cut in with chilling softness at Beth's deliberate use of that name he found so offensive. 'Now if you will kindly remove yourself—'

'I told you, we're not going anywhere until I get to the bottom of this mystery.' Beth was glaring up at him until their noses almost touched.

It was too much for Grace.

Far, far too much.

She began to laugh, inappropriate and slightly hysterical humour that caused both Cesar and Beth to turn and look at her, Beth irritably, Cesar angrily. 'I'm sorry,' Grace finally managed to choke out. 'It's just— If the two of you could only see— You look so— Esther…?' She turned to the older woman for assistance.

Esther drew in a deep and steadying breath, her smile

one of tremulous wonder. 'I believe, as does Grace—' she briefly turned that tearful smile on Grace before turning back to look at Cesar and Beth with glowing eyes '—that—'

'*Esther, que—*'

'Carlos!' Esther turned to hold out her hand to her husband as he stood in the doorway behind her. 'Come, Carlos,' she encouraged emotionally, taking his hand in hers when he moved to her side, before raising that hand to her lips and kissing his knuckles. 'I believe I may have just witnessed a miracle, my love. The first argument between our son and our daughter,' she explained as that 'son and daughter' continued to look at her with equally stubbornly angry faces.

Stubbornly angry faces that could surely be none other than those of Cesar Navarro and his young sister, Gabriela?

CHAPTER TWELEVE

'WHY IS IT THAT I ALWAYS find you in the kitchen?'

Grace turned sharply at the sound of Cesar's voice behind her, the muted light on over the stove to break the darkness of the kitchen. The same kitchen where only days ago she had prepared Cesar's birthday dinner. So much had happened since that night, it seemed a lifetime ago.

She eyed him warily. 'Probably because it's the place I'm most comfortable.'

'Please do not get up.' Cesar nodded as she would have risen from sitting on one of the stools at the breakfast bar. 'I—could not sleep, either.'

'It's been an unusual evening.' Grace grimaced at her understatement.

Unusual didn't even begin to describe the strangeness of the past few hours. A time of conversations begun but never finished. Of questions that seemed to have no answers. Of Esther and Carlos Navarro sitting together on one of the sofas holding hands as they stared intently at Beth, as if they were both afraid to believe she might possibly be their long-lost daughter—which no doubt they were, and perhaps quite rightly so.

Cesar had left the room to make some telephone calls, and managed to arrange for DNA tests to be carried out the following day, and in the meantime Esther and Carlos had insisted that Grace and Beth couldn't possibly stay at a hotel, but must both come here, to Cesar's apartment, at least until after they had received the results of the blood tests.

Cesar had spent the rest of the evening looking at Grace in brooding silence, as if he somehow thought he might find the answers to his own questions in her face.

Answers Grace hadn't had then, and certainly didn't have now, several hours later. She genuinely didn't know if Beth was the missing Gabriela Navarro—the longer the evening went on, the more she had wondered if she hadn't just imagined all of those coincidences. If she hadn't managed to convince herself that it was possible Beth could be Gabriela, because she had wanted to take away Cesar's pain and that of his parents. Cesar had been right earlier: the coincidences, and Beth's likeness to Gabriela, were purely cosmetic—

'Carla Lawrence, Beth's mother, was Argentinian by birth.'

She blinked at Cesar. 'Sorry?'

Cesar stepped further into the light, revealing that he wore a white tee shirt and soft cotton jogging trousers that fitted low down on his hips; the clothes he wore to sleep in? Probably, Grace realized. After all, he hadn't expected to find anyone else in the kitchen.

He grimaced. 'When I left to call the doctor earlier I also instructed Raphael to begin an investigation into Beth's real parents. Obviously there is a time difference between our two countries, which is slowing things down slightly, but so far he has found out that Carla Lawrence was of Argentinian extraction.'

Grace swallowed hard before speaking. 'Is that a good or bad thing, do you think?'

'What I think is that it is a coincidence that requires further investigation,' Cesar answered softly.

Another coincidence, he could have said, but didn't. Because they both knew that at this point in time, that was all any of these things were: coincidences...

'Cesar, I'm sorry. I'm really sorry.' Tears blurred Grace's vision as she looked across the breakfast bar at him. 'I just—I saw that photograph of Gabriela in your bedroom, and the likeness to Beth was so startling—' She gave a shake of her head. 'I— Beth didn't want to come here. She honestly thinks I've gone crazy. I should have at least called you first and—'

'And risked being rejected out of hand,' he finished. 'You did the right thing, Grace. You did the only thing that someone of your nature could have done.'

'My nature?' Grace stiffened warily.

'You have a kindness, a caring for other people's happiness which has nothing to do with your own.' He nodded. 'Which, in this case, has manifested itself into an empathy of understanding for the pain suffered by both myself and my parents in regard to Gabriela's disappearance.'

'Oh.'

'Not what you expected me to say, hmm?'

'Not quite.' She grimaced, having been prepared to face Cesar's anger, the same anger he had expressed earlier, the next time they found themselves alone together.

'I was upset earlier.' Cesar seemed to guess her thoughts. 'Said things, made accusations, I should not have made. Beth was right—I should not have spoken to you in the way that I did. Despite my initial response, and even if it should be that Beth is not my sister after all, I will always feel...grateful to you for at least bringing this likeness to our attention,' he added huskily. 'For once again giving my mother hope.'

Gratitude. No matter what happened, Grace would always have Cesar's gratitude. When she wanted so much more from him. When she felt so much more for him. When just to be with him again made her heart ache. 'That's good.' She attempted a brief smile, hoping that she looked more convincing than she felt. 'How long do you think it will take Raphael to complete his investigation?'

Cesar quirked dark brows. 'You are in a hurry to leave Argentina?'

She gave a rueful shake of her head. 'I probably shouldn't have come back here in the first place. Or brought Beth with me. She argued, told me the whole idea was ridiculous but— I don't know what I was thinking—'

'As I said, you were thinking of others, not yourself,' Cesar cut in firmly. 'Although, I agree, Beth is not at all appreciative of that sentiment at the moment!' he added dryly.

Grace gave a husky laugh. 'Watching the two of you standing virtually nose to nose earlier tonight was pretty amazing.'

He nodded. 'Not at all how I had envisaged—if, as my mother said, by some miracle it should turn out that Beth is Gabriela, after all!—my first meeting with my little sister in twenty-one years!'

Grace gave another choked laugh. 'It was explosive, to say the least. Our parents brought us up to stand up for ourselves, as well as others, no matter what the situation,' she added apologetically.

'And Beth did not at all appreciate the way in which I had spoken to her sister.'

'No, she's certainly keeping a wary eye on you, buster!' Beth drawled as she strolled into the kitchen, blonde hair secured in a ponytail, her face cleansed of make-up and looking vulnerably young, her night attire almost a mirror image of Cesar's.

Cesar quirked a dark brow. 'Is "buster" an improvement on "buddy", or worse?'

'Depends on whether or not you're upsetting my big sister,' she came back pertly.

Cesar frowned. 'If you should indeed be Gabriela, this could all become rather complicated; what would my relationship then be to Grace?'

Grace stiffened. 'I—'

'Whatever she decides it's going to be,' Beth spoke firmly. 'Anyone else for coffee?' she offered as she poured the water into the percolator and added coffee.

Grace was still a little thrown by Cesar's question, let alone Beth's answer, and could only nod distractedly at the same time as Cesar murmured his own affirmation as he continued to watch Beth through narrowed lids as she prepared the coffee.

What would Grace's relationship to Cesar be if it transpired that her adopted sister was his missing sister, Gabriela?

It was too late at night, and emotions were running too high, the question too complicated, for Grace to be able to think straight on that particular subject!

'Here we— Damn it!' Beth swore even as one of the mugs of coffee slipped from her fingers.

'Move, Brela!' Cesar reacted quickly enough to push Beth out of the way as the mug hit the marble floor and shattered into pieces, at the same time as scalding-hot coffee sprayed everywhere. 'Both of you stay exactly where you are!' he instructed the women harshly even as he crouched down to begin picking up the pieces of broken china prior to mopping up the spilt coffee.

'Beth?'

Cesar straightened as he heard the concern in Grace's

voice. 'Did the coffee burn you?' He frowned darkly at the younger of the two Blake sisters.

Beth gave a slow shake of her head, her cheeks having gone very pale as she stared at him. 'What did you just call me?'

He gave a puzzled shake of his head. 'I do not recall—'

'Brela,' Grace put in softly, her concerned gaze still fixed on Beth. 'He called you Brela.'

'I did not realise… It was the name by which I always called Gabriela,' Cesar supplied slowly.

Beth swallowed. 'I don't— For just a moment I thought it sounded— No, it couldn't have been,' she dismissed briskly. 'No one remembers things from when they were two years old.'

'I do,' Cesar assured her abruptly.

Beth raised her eyes heavenwards. 'Why am I not surprised?'

'Beth!' Grace admonished exasperatedly.

'Well, honestly!' Beth muttered deprecatingly before turning back to Cesar. 'The man is a damned machine— If you called your sister, Brela, what did she call you?' She eyed him warily.

'She could not pronounce Cesar properly and so she called me—'

'Zar,' Beth provided softly.

'Yes,' Cesar confirmed in a hushed voice.

Her creamy brow creased in concentration for several seconds before she came back tartly, 'Must have been a lucky guess.'

'Was it?' he prompted softly.

'Well, it had to be, didn't it?' Beth dismissed impatiently. 'As I said, no one—apart from Cesar Navarro, obviously!—remembers things from when they were two years old!'

'You—'

'Are you aware that the two of you are doing it again?' Grace couldn't help but smile ruefully as two pairs of identical brown eyes turned to glare at her. 'You're squabbling like a couple of children,' she explained patiently. 'Or siblings,' she added pensively.

Beth looked positively mutinous. 'Esther and Carlos are really nice people, but I'm not sure I could cope with learning I have someone this overbearing as an older brother.'

'Beth!' Grace gasped in dismay, only to turn and look at Cesar in alarm as he began to laugh. And kept on laughing.

Which was something of a miracle in itself. Cesar laughing—brown eyes glowing with that humour, all harshness wiped from his expression, even white teeth gleaming between his parted lips—was even more disturbing, more sexy, than when the two of them had danced the tango together.

'I don't see what's so funny,' Beth muttered bad-temperedly when it seemed Cesar wasn't going to stop laughing.

He sobered enough to speak. 'You are just as outspoken about the faults you perceive in my character as your sister is!' He continued to chuckle.

'That's probably because—'

'And just as cranky when you don't get enough sleep.' Grace spoke firmly as she stood up and took a determined hold of her sister's arm. 'Time for bed, Beth. Before you insult our host any further.' She shot Cesar an apologetic glance; if he and Beth should turn out to be brother and sister, then it promised to be a very stormy relationship.

'He set the tone for our conversations when he was so rude to you when we arrived—'

'Beth, please.'

'Okay, okay, I'll go to bed,' her sister huffed. 'Just keep

your hands off my sister.' She shot Cesar a warning glance as she picked up her coffee mug before striding out of the kitchen.

Grace had intended accompanying Beth, rather than being left alone in the kitchen with Cesar when her sister—their sister?—stomped off.

Instead Grace turned to give Cesar an apologetic grimace. 'I really do apologise for Beth's behaviour. She—she's actually more upset about all of this than she wants people to know.'

Cesar nodded. 'And you? How will you feel if it should turn out that Beth is really Brela?'

Her brow creased into a frown. 'It was really odd the way she seemed to recognise that name, don't you think?'

'How will you feel about it, Grace?' he persisted. 'About me?'

Grace was pretty sure that Cesar hadn't been standing this close to her a few seconds ago. So close that she could smell his aftershave, and feel the heat of his body, seducing her, enticing her—

She shook off her sudden feeling of lethargy as she straightened determinedly. 'It's a little soon to ask that, don't you think? After all—'

'I have missed you this past three days, Grace,' Cesar cut in huskily as he smoothed a wisp of dark hair back from her cheek. 'More than I would ever have believed it possible to miss anyone,' he added gruffly.

Grace gave him a quick glance, and then wished she hadn't as she saw that the warmth of his gaze was fixed on her parted lips. Lips she nervously moistened with the tip of her tongue before answering him. 'No one to challenge you or answer you back, hmm?' she attempted to lighten the sudden tension in the room.

'No one to challenge me or answer me back,' he confirmed softly. 'Or to dance the tango with me. Or to take me from my ivory tower to smell the roses. Grace—'

'Cesar, no matter how this might look, I really didn't come back here to have our conversation,' she interrupted quickly as she began edging away from him. 'Emotions are running high, uncertainty mixed in with a certain amount of hope—'

'You believe I am only saying these things to you because you may—and that is still a very big may—have returned Gabriela to us?'

'Why else?' she dismissed lightly. 'And quite frankly, I don't—'

'Do you honestly believe that it is gratitude for returning that hellion to us—if indeed Beth should turn out to be Gabriela—that makes me speak to you in this way?' he continued dryly.

Grace gave a wince. 'I told you, Beth is as tense about all of this as you obviously are. She isn't usually as acerbic as she's been to you since she arrived.'

'Or perhaps she sensed just now that, once she had left us alone together, it was my intention to seduce her big sister into sharing my bed tonight rather than occupying the second single bed in her own bedroom?'

Grace's eyes widened as Cesar's arms moved about her waist and he tugged her close against his lean and muscled length, the hard outline of his arousal pressing against her softness. 'It was?'

Cesar lowered his head until his lips could taste the sweet length of her throat. 'It still is,' he corrected softly.

'I— This isn't a good idea, Cesar.' Even as she protested Grace's back arched in pleasure.

He looked down at her searchingly as he slowly released her before stepping back. 'Did you not listen just now when I said that I have missed you, Grace?' he finally murmured softly.

She blinked. 'You sent me back to England.'

'I thought it was for the best at the time. That the circumstances merited we spend some time apart in order to see where, or if, our relationship progressed any further.' His nostrils flared as he breathed in deeply. 'It was a decision I regretted almost as soon as I had made it.'

'Because our lovemaking was interrupted the other day.' She nodded in understanding. 'But that—that behaviour really isn't me, Cesar. We had just spent an enjoyable day together, and dancing the tango together was—'

'Erotic,' he provided huskily.

'To say the least.' Grace became slightly flustered at the admission. 'But I'm really not the sort of woman who wants to become the mistress of a powerful entrepreneur businessman who's worth billions, if not zillions.' Even one she now knew she was very in love with!

One look at Cesar earlier, being with him again, close to him, and Grace knew that was exactly what had happened to her. She was in love with Cesar Navarro. A love that could only lead to despair, if not complete heartbreak! The same love that had brought her to Buenos Aires on what she now suspected was a wild goose chase...

CHAPTER THIRTEEN

CESAR'S BROWS ARCHED up into his hairline. 'Is that what you think of me?' he said slowly. 'That after all you have done—tried to do—for both my family and me—that I now wish to make you my mistress?'

'What else?' she said again.

'You do not think that perhaps I could have feelings for you?'

Grace's heart leapt in her chest, and then as quickly fell. Of course Cesar didn't have feelings for her. Well, not beyond desire, at least. He hadn't even been pleased to see her again when she had arrived earlier!

'No, I don't,' she said dryly. 'And, despite what you might think to the contrary, I don't do affairs.'

She might have been carried away the other day, might have let things go further between herself and Cesar than they ever had with any other man, but she really couldn't become his mistress for the short time it would take for him to tire of her. Cesar might never be photographed escorting beautiful women but Grace had no doubts, after their lovemaking four days ago, that he was a very experienced lover, and that he hadn't become that way by remaining celibate. Whereas Grace— Her lovemaking with Cesar had been with his encouragement and instruction, and otherwise completely instinctive rather than experienced, and she seriously doubted that Cesar would appreciate having a complete innocent in his bed, even for a short time.

Or that he would ever grow to love her in the way that she now knew she loved him. Wholeheartedly, and completely.

She drew herself up determinedly. 'I really think it's for the best if I go to bed now. And no matter what happens tomorrow—'

'Yes?' Cesar prompted as Grace broke off abruptly.

She drew in a deep breath. 'No matter what happens tomorrow, what the blood tests prove or disprove, the intimacies we've shared, does not mean we ever had a relationship.'

Cesar gave a tight smile. 'Beth appears to have other ideas.'

'Not because of anything I've told her, I assure you.'

'You do not need to reassure me of anything, Grace,' he said softly. 'Nor would it be unacceptable for you to have discussed with your sister our...having been together, before you returned to England.'

'Well, I didn't. And I haven't. She just seems to have added two and two together.'

'And come to the correct conclusion that the two of us are involved,' Cesar finished softly.

Grace shook her head. 'Beth, despite the appearances to the contrary, is a romantic.'

'And you are not?'

'A believer in happy-ever-after?' She quirked dark brows. 'Of course,' she conceded ruefully. 'But not to the point of believing in fairy tales.'

'And, in your opinion, a relationship between the two of us would be a fairy tale?' Cesar watched her closely.

'A meaningful relationship between billionaire Cesar

Navarro and his temporary cook/housekeeper would most definitely be a fairy tale!' she drawled dryly.

Cesar frowned his irritation. 'And what if they were to fall in love with each other?'

She gave a tense start. 'That isn't going to happen.'

'Why not?'

'For all the reasons I've previously stated!'

'The only reason I recall of any significance—to you, that is—is that I am a billionaire, you are currently my cook/housekeeper.' Cesar eyed her questioningly.

'And you have affairs and I don't.' Her cheeks became flushed.

He raised dark brows. 'Says who?'

'Well— I— You…' Grace gave an impatient shake of her head. 'This is a ridiculous conversation, Cesar.'

'I agree,' he drawled. 'It is beyond ridiculous.' He scowled. 'Grace, you will not always be my cook/housekeeper.'

'And?'

'And we talked once of the possibility of you owning and running your own restaurant. I could help you achieve your dream.'

'Please stop,' Grace cut in warningly, her eyes flashing the colour of turquoise. 'I'm not for sale.'

'I am not offering to buy you, Grace.' Cesar's voice was a low growl, his eyes narrowed slits.

Her chin rose stubbornly. 'Then what are you offering?'

'I am suggesting that you might consider marrying me first, and then opening your own restaurant.'

'Marrying you!' Grace repeated incredulously. 'How did we go from "I'm not for sale" to "marry me"?'

Cesar's mouth firmed. 'We did not. You are the one who talked of affairs and mistresses,' he corrected. 'I never, at any time in our conversation, so much as implied I wished for either of those things with you.'

'Maybe not, but...' Grace's cheeks were very pale. 'Cesar, you can't be serious about wanting to marry me!'

His jaw tightened. 'I am very serious.'

'Because Beth might be your sister and it might prove awkward if we were to decide to continue—'

'No one else has any relevance to this conversation but the two of us!' His eyes glittered darkly in his impatience. 'Grace, I—I realised after you had left Buenos Aires that I—I have fallen in love with you. I intended talking to you, telling you how much I love you, as soon as I returned to England, and hoped that you might feel something for me in return.' He frowned as she stumbled back a step to place her hand on the breakfast bar for support. 'Is that so impossible, Grace?'

'I— No, of course it isn't.'

He looked relieved. 'It was not my intention to propose to you in the kitchen, dressed only in my nightclothes, but—' Humour now lightened his expression. 'As you said earlier, it is the place you feel most comfortable, so perhaps it is not so ridiculous, after all.'

Grace moistened the dryness of her lips. 'Proposing to me?'

Cesar went down on one knee on the tiled floor before reaching out to take her free hand in both of his. 'Grace Blake, will you consider marrying me?'

'I—I...'

'Will you please marry me, Grace?' Cesar continued determinedly. 'Please love me? Will you be at my side for the rest of our lives? Will you have babies with me?' His eyes glowed darkly. 'Beautiful sable-haired babies with green-blue eyes? I love you so much, Grace! Please marry me and I promise that you will never regret it.'

Grace could barely breathe as she stared down at him in wide-eyed wonder. 'I— You don't know anything about me...'

He smiled up at her. 'I know everything about you that is important. You have a beauty which is not skin deep but flows into your heart and your mind, and encompasses everyone around you. I also know that you are totally loyal, to your family, friends, and even to billionaire Argentinian businessmen, who have done nothing to deserve that loyalty!' He smiled slightly. 'I also know that you are adopted, that you loved your adoptive parents but wish to also know who your birth parents were—and we will find them, Grace, I promise you that,' he assured her gruffly. 'I also know that you are an innocent.'

'How can you possibly know that?' Grace gasped, the rest of what Cesar was saying to her too fantastic—too unexpected—for her to completely take it in. Yet... 'Was I so awful the other day?'

'You were exquisite, Grace,' Cesar assured her gruffly. 'Absolutely exquisite. So much so that I cannot wait to make love with you again.' He reached up to touch the curve of her cheek. 'But you are an innocent, Grace. And I love you for it.' He smiled gently. 'I, too, am a virgin of sorts— But I am, Grace,' he continued softly as she gave a disbelieving snort. 'I do not deny that I have had physical relationships—how could I?—but I had never made love with a woman before you.'

Love. Cesar really was telling her that he loved her. That he wanted to marry her.

Grace swallowed hard. 'Are you absolutely sure this is what you want, Cesar? I'm not from your world. I have no idea how to be the wife of a billionaire businessman.'

'An Argentinian billionaire businessman, specifically Cesar Navarro,' he corrected huskily. 'And we will make our own world in whatever way you are comfortable. You are all that I want, Grace,' he assured her softly. 'All I will ever want. The woman I wish to dance the tango with for the rest of my life. The woman with whom I wish to "smell the roses". If you do not love me yet—'

'How could I not love you—?' She broke off, her cheeks flushing with colour. 'Of course I love you, Cesar,' she assured him huskily. 'I love you very much. So much...' Her voice broke emotionally as she looked down at him with that love shining in her eyes. 'I'm just afraid...'

'Of what?' His hand tightened on hers. 'Tell me what you are afraid of, Grace, and I will do everything in my power to take away that fear.'

'I'm afraid I'll let you down! That I won't fit in. I don't belong in this world, Cesar.' She looked around at the opulence of the room. 'I don't belong in your world!'

'A world of security cameras and security guards.' He nodded gravely. 'You know the reason for them now, but if you really cannot live with them then they will all go.'

'All of them?'

Cesar smiled ruefully at her dazed expression. 'All. If you agree to marry me, then I will have my fierce and loyal wife by my side. And, as I have told you, Raphael and I are agreed that no one would dare challenge her.'

Grace gave a shake of her head. 'You're teasing me now, Cesar.'

'Because I am nervous.' He looked up at her intently. 'And because I am still on my knees on the kitchen floor waiting for you to answer my proposal of marriage!'

'Beth—'

'Has absolutely nothing to do with us, here and now,' Cesar assured her firmly. 'Yes, I searched for Gabriela for years, before I gave that search up as futile. Yes, I have missed her every day since she was taken. And yes, I would welcome even your hellion of a sister if it is really Gabriela returned to us at last. But you are the only thing that is important to me now, Grace. You, and only you.'

Grace looked down at him searchingly, unable to deny the love she saw shining in those dark, expressive eyes as they met hers unblinkingly. Love for her. Only her. 'Oh, Cesar.'

'Grace?'

She breathed shakily. 'I do love you, Cesar. I believe I started to fall in love with you before we left England, but I definitely fell fully in love with you the day we spent walking around Buenos Aires together.'

'And?'

She winced. 'Marriage, Cesar?'

'I will settle for nothing less.'

She could see that he meant what he said, by the determined glitter in his eyes, and the stubborn set of his jaw. 'Where would we live?'

'Wherever we are together we will call home.'

'Oh, Cesar, that was exactly the right answer!' She reached up to touch that stubbornly set jaw even as the tears of happiness blurred her vision. 'I feel the same way, my love,' she assured him emotionally. 'And my answer is yes. Yes, I'll marry you, Cesar. Yes, I'll be your wife. Yes, I'll spend the rest of my life with you, and yes, I'll give you sable-haired green-eyed babies. Yes, yes, yes!'

She launched herself into his waiting arms.

'You do realise that my mother is going to insist on helping you plan the wedding?' Cesar murmured softly a long time later as he carried Grace down the silent hallway.

'I would really love that.' Grace glowed up at him, the love she felt for him shining brightly in her eyes as her arms encircled his neck.

Cesar smiled down at her. 'And you will make the wedding soon?'

She looked up at him teasingly. 'How soon?'

He raised dark brows. 'Tomorrow will not be soon enough for me.'

Grace gave a happy laugh. 'I think it might take a little longer to organise than that.'

'Make it soon, Grace,' he pressed gruffly. 'And afterwards, your restaurant?'

'Maybe one day— Why have you stopped here?' She gave Cesar a puzzled look as he came to a halt outside the bedroom she was sharing with Beth.

Cesar lowered her regretfully to her feet. 'I dearly wish for you to wear white on our wedding day, which means we will have to sleep apart until we are married.'

'But—'

'Unless you feel we could share a bed without making love?' he added teasingly.

'Could you?'

His eyes darkened. 'No more than a snowball could survive in hell! No,' he breathed raggedly, a nerve pulsing in his clenched jaw. 'No, Grace, I could not. I love you too much, want you too much, to be able to resist you if you were in my bed and in my arms.'

'I feel the same way,' she admitted huskily. 'So, separate beds it is until our wedding day.' She looked up at Cesar curiously as he began to smile as he glanced towards the closed bedroom door behind her. 'What's so funny?'

'Beth's reaction to our news.' He grinned openly now. 'Gabriela or not, she is not going to be at all pleased to learn that she is going to have me as her "overbearing" brother-in-law!'

'You have a decidedly wicked streak in you, Mr Navarro!' Grace chuckled softly. 'But I love you for it.'

'As I love you.' He kissed her gently. 'And that, my darling Grace, is all that matters.'

And it was.

Whatever answers tomorrow might bring, confirmation or denial of Beth being Gabriela Navarro, Grace knew a complete confidence in Cesar's love for her. Just as she had absolutely no doubts that she and Cesar would spend the rest of their lives in love and loving each other, that any problems they might have in the future they would work out.

Together.

* * * * *

COMING NEXT MONTH from Harlequin Presents®
AVAILABLE APRIL 23, 2013

#3137 A RICH MAN'S WHIM
A Bride for a Billionaire
Lynne Graham

Bedding Kat should be easy for billionaire Mikhail, but the tempting redhead is impossible to seduce! So Mikhail offers to pay off her debts—in exchange for a month on his yacht, and in his cabin, virginity included!

#3138 A LEGACY OF SECRETS
Sicily's Corretti Dynasty
Carol Marinelli

P.A. to the infamous Santo Corretti, Ella is run ragged fielding the playboy's heartbroken exes. But his film's director quits, and Ella steps in, proving her capabilities extend beyond the morning coffee run. Soon Santo's offering her overtime...after hours.

#3139 A TOUCH OF NOTORIETY
Buenos Aires Nights
Carole Mortimer

Beth Blake had a normal life in London until a secret thrust her into worldwide notoriety. Now she's in Argentina, guarded by Raphael Cordoba—controlling, insufferable and sinfully sexy to boot, will she be able to resist this illicit temptation?

#3140 MAID FOR MONTERO
At His Service
Kim Lawrence

Isandro Montero can't believe that his new housekeeper is so inept! She must go. Except firing beautiful Zoe would ruin his reputation, so he'll put Zoe where he can keep his eyes on her...and maybe his hands—in his bed!

You can find more information on upcoming Harlequin®
titles, free excerpts and more at www.Harlequin.com.

HPCNM0413RA

#3141 HEIR TO A DARK INHERITANCE
Secret Heirs of Powerful Men
Maisey Yates

Jada will do anything to keep her daughter in her life, even marry the man whose heart is said to be carved from diamonds and cold as ice. There's no future for them, but resisting the powerful Alik is impossible.

#3142 THE SECRET CASELLA BABY
Cathy Williams

In one night, ordinary girl Holly goes from nobody to celebrity! Pregnant with notorious billionaire Luiz Casella's baby, she'll have to get used to living among the rich and famous.... A Casella heir *cannot* be born out of wedlock!

#3143 A PRICE WORTH PAYING?
Trish Morey

Their marriage might unite their warring families, but formidable Spaniard Alesander Esquivel is the last man on earth beautiful Simone would want to be in the same room as—let alone share a marital bed! Isn't he?

#3144 CAPTIVE IN HIS CASTLE
Chantelle Shaw

Drago knows that Jess is a thief and a liar, so to protect his family, he'll keep her close. But captive in his palazzo, Jess gets under his skin—and their anger soon turns to fiery passion!

REQUEST YOUR FREE BOOKS!

2 FREE NOVELS PLUS
2 FREE GIFTS!

YES! Please send me 2 FREE Harlequin Presents® novels and my 2 FREE gifts (gifts are worth about $10). After receiving them, if I don't wish to receive any more books, I can return the shipping statement marked "cancel." If I don't cancel, I will receive 6 brand-new novels every month and be billed just $4.30 per book in the U.S. or $4.99 per book in Canada. That's a saving of at least 14% off the cover price! It's quite a bargain! Shipping and handling is just 50¢ per book in the U.S. and 75¢ per book in Canada.* I understand that accepting the 2 free books and gifts places me under no obligation to buy anything. I can always return a shipment and cancel at any time. Even if I never buy another book, the two free books and gifts are mine to keep forever.

106/306 HDN FVRK

Name	(PLEASE PRINT)
Address	Apt. #
City	State/Prov.	Zip/Postal Code

Signature (if under 18, a parent or guardian must sign)

Mail to the **Harlequin® Reader Service:**
IN U.S.A.: P.O. Box 1867, Buffalo, NY 14240-1867
IN CANADA: P.O. Box 609, Fort Erie, Ontario L2A 5X3

**Are you a current subscriber to Harlequin Presents books
and want to receive the larger-print edition?
Call 1-800-873-8635 or visit www.ReaderService.com.**

* Terms and prices subject to change without notice. Prices do not include applicable taxes. Sales tax applicable in N.Y. Canadian residents will be charged applicable taxes. Offer not valid in Quebec. This offer is limited to one order per household. Not valid for current subscribers to Harlequin Presents books. All orders subject to credit approval. Credit or debit balances in a customer's account(s) may be offset by any other outstanding balance owed by or to the customer. Please allow 4 to 6 weeks for delivery. Offer available while quantities last.

Your Privacy—The Harlequin® Reader Service is committed to protecting your privacy. Our Privacy Policy is available online at www.ReaderService.com or upon request from the Harlequin Reader Service.

We make a portion of our mailing list available to reputable third parties that offer products we believe may interest you. If you prefer that we not exchange your name with third parties, or if you wish to clarify or modify your communication preferences, please visit us at www.ReaderService.com/consumerschoice or write to us at Harlequin Reader Service Preference Service, P.O. Box 9062, Buffalo, NY 14269. Include your complete name and address.

Discover the empire, the scandal and the legacy…

SICILY'S CORRETTI DYNASTY

The more powerful the family…the darker the secrets!

Behind the closed doors of their opulent palazzo, ruthless
desire and the lethal Corretti charm are alive and well.
Young, rich and notoriously handsome, the Correttis'
legendary exploits regularly feature in Sicily's tabloid pages!
But no disgrace or scandal will stand in their way….

Harlequin Presents invites you to enter the
Corretti family's dark and dazzling world.

Collect all eight passionate new tales written by
USA TODAY **bestselling authors, beginning May 2013.**

A LEGACY OF SECRETS—Carol Marinelli (May)

AN INVITATION TO SIN—Sarah Morgan (June)

A SHADOW OF GUILT—Abby Green (July)

AN INHERITANCE OF SHAME—Kate Hewitt (August)

A WHISPER OF DISGRACE—Sharon Kendrick (September)

A FACADE TO SHATTER—Lynn Raye Harris (October)

A SCANDAL IN THE HEADLINES—Caitlin Crews (November)

A HUNGER FOR THE FORBIDDEN—Maisey Yates (December)